He was the right man, but something was wrong

"Niall, please," Joss persisted, "can't you tell me what your trouble is?" Her voice was almost smothered in his chest as she went on. "No matter what it is, I'll do my best to understand."

"I can't, Joss—it's too late. And it wouldn't be fair," he said, his voice sober.

"What you're doing to me now is hardly fair!"

"I warned you yesterday this is the way it would be. Tomorrow I may well kick myself for being so noble, but that's the way I have to play it."

Joss pulled back to search his face for the slightest sign of relenting—and found none.

SANDRA FIELD, once a biology technician, now writes full-time under the pen names of Jocelyn Haley and Jan MacLean. She lives with her son in Canada's Maritimes, which she often uses as a setting for her books. She loves the independent life-style she has as a writer. She's her own boss, sets her own hours, and increasingly there are travel opportunities.

Books by Sandra Field

HARLEQUIN PRESENTS

768—A CHANGE OF HEART
799—OUT OF WEDLOCK
824—A WORLD OF DIFFERENCE
905—ONE IN A MILLION
977—AN IDEAL MATCH
1034—SINGLE COMBAT
1120—LOVE IN A MIST

HARLEQUIN ROMANCE

2457—THE STORMS OF SPRING
2480—SIGHT OF A STRANGER
2577—THE TIDES OF SUMMER
1159—CHASE A RAINBOW

writing as Jan MacLean

2295—EARLY SUMMER
2348—WHITE FIRE
2547—ALL OUR TOMORROWS

writing as Jocelyn Haley

DREAM OF DARKNESS

HARLEQUIN SUPERROMANCE

217—A TIME TO LOVE
254—DRIVE THE NIGHT AWAY

Don't miss any of our special offers. Write to us at the following address for information on our newest releases.

Harlequin Reader Service
901 Fuhrmann Blvd., P.O. Box 1397, Buffalo, NY 14240
Canadian address: P.O. Box 603,
Fort Erie, Ont. L2A 5X3

SANDRA FIELD

the right man

Harlequin Books

TORONTO • NEW YORK • LONDON
AMSTERDAM • PARIS • SYDNEY • HAMBURG
STOCKHOLM • ATHENS • TOKYO • MILAN

Harlequin Presents first edition June 1989
ISBN 0-373-11178-9

Original hardcover edition published in 1988
by Mills & Boon Limited

PROLOGUE

'ONE day you'll meet the right man,' Ellie MacDougal had repeatedly told her youngest daughter Joss, ever since the time when Joss had become interested in the opposite sex as something other than rowdy members of the baseball team. 'You'll know him right away. And that will be that.'

Joss had always had great faith in her mother's predictions, for Ellie combined sound Scottish common sense with a wild streak of romanticism, inherited from a Moravian gypsy who had very briefly, but entirely legally, been married to Ellie's grandfather. Besides, Ellie's own marriage gave credence to her predictions. Ellie had met George MacDougall at a church social forty years ago, had altered the place settings so he would sit beside her, and had married him six months later. 'The minute I saw him I knew he was the man for me,' she had told Joss on more than one occasion. 'It took him a little while to come round. But I convinced him in the end.' And she would toss her greying curls, and her eyes, dark as any gypsy's, would laugh at Joss. 'You'll see, the same thing will happen to you. You'll walk into a room some day and this man will look over at you, and bingo—you'll be lost!'

Secretly Joss pictured the scenario quite differently. She would meet her unknown lover on her father's farm in the springtime. She would be wandering through the orchard wearing a filmy white dress and a floppy hat bordered with flowers, and the sky would be blue and the air fragrant with the scent of apple blossoms; in her daydream she always managed to ignore the presence of the dandelions that bloomed at the same time as the apple trees, for dandelions did not seem the flowers of romance. But the grass would swish around her ankles and the bees would hum drowsily on the pale pink petals and then she would see him, standing further up the slope, waiting for her, her handsome, blue-eyed lover . . .

And here the daydream would end, for Joss could never quite picture the man's features. The blue eyes she was sure of, for they would complement her own eyes, which were hazel, flecked with gold. But was he blond, a lighter blond than her own tawny, sun-streaked curls? Or dark, hair black as the wings of the crows that nested in the elm trees west of the orchard? But crows, like dandelions, were not very romantic, and with a sigh Joss would return to the real world and abandon her imaginary lover, the man who was the right man for her, the only man in the whole wide world.

At the age of seventeen she left the village of Alderney in western Nova Scotia where she had lived on the farm with her four brothers and two sisters, and went to university in Halifax. She had grown up knowing what hard work was all about, so she obtained an honours degree in biology and chemistry without a great deal of difficulty; she sang a leading role each year in the musical put on by the drama club, and she dated a lot, for she was pretty and outgoing. Although she met several blue-eyed young men, none of them struck her to the heart; however, she was having enough fun that the omission did not trouble her. And every spring when the orchard burst into bloom she would remember, with an inward smile, her adolescent, romantic dream. At the advanced age of twenty-one she was still convinced that somehow she would meet the man who was her destiny in the way that she had always imagined.

CHAPTER ONE

JOSS was late for work. Again. She scurried along the pavement, from long practice dodging the tourists, the punk kids bedecked with chains, and the street vendors. Rock music blared from a shop front. A car horn blasted in her ear. Yonge Street in Toronto on a hot Wednesday in August . . . would Dante's Inferno be very much different? she wondered grimly, feeling her blouse stick to her back as she waited for the traffic light to change. She had been working at the bookshop all day, and in theory got off at four. But Cathy, her replacement, had been twenty minutes late for the second time in the past week, which meant that Joss now had exactly twenty-five minutes to get back from the bookshop to the hotel where she sang in the bar every evening from five until nine. She hated being late. She hated rushing. She hated Toronto in August.

Joss blinked rapidly, trying to blame the sudden stinging in her eyes on exhaust fumes. At that precise moment she would have given every cent she had saved all summer to be back in the orchard at home, where the grass was green, the fruit was ripening, and the tang of the distant ocean tantalised the nostrils. The Guernseys would be grazing in the meadow. Her mother's chickens would be clucking in their pen. The cats would be sleeping in the sun and Bert, the old collie, would be watching them from the corner of his eye; from long experience the cats knew Bert was too lazy to do anything other than watch.

The light changed. The crowd surged across the street, carrying Joss with them. She edged between a

7

very fat lady and a tall young man in flowered shorts, and began to run. Mr Jodrey, who was the manager of the Red Lion Pub in the Swansea Hotel, was a stickler for punctuality.

By the time she arrived at the side entrance of the Swansea it was five to five. In the staff room she splashed cold water on her face, peeled off her cotton trousers and shirt, daubed herself with perfume and struggled into the embroidered peasant blouse and frilly green skirt that Mr Jodrey had provided for her; at the very beginning of the summer Joss had decided that her gypsy grandmother would have scorned so cute an outfit. She ran a brush through her hair, tried to disguise the shininess of her nose with powder, and outlined her lips in a soft apricot lipstick. Then, taking her time, she removed her guitar from its case and replaced the case in her locker. The guitar had belonged to her great-aunt on her mother's side. Great-Aunt Lucy, who had had lustrous dark hair and snapping black eyes, had run off with a travelling salesman and had died in a train crash under circumstances that had never been fully explained. Joss loved the guitar for its burnished wood and clarity of tone, and for its tie to an ancestry that sometimes, unexpectedly, would sing in her blood.

She took a quick glance at herself in the mirror, hitched up the waistband of her skirt, and left the room. Various corridors led from the staff room to the kitchen, the lifts and the basements; the one that Joss took underwent a sudden transformation past a pair of swing doors from linoleum and dull beige paint to rose carpeting and wallpaper. She hurried past the cloakrooms intended for the use of visitors to the bar, turned the corner, and saw the man a fraction of a second before he collided with her. Her action was instinctive: she thrust the guitar away from her to protect it from the impact and ran full into his chest.

'Oh! Do be careful!' she gasped, two seconds too late. Then she looked up.

The man had blue eyes.

As though she was fitting together the pieces of a jigsaw puzzle, Joss saw that his hair was so dark a brown as to be almost black, that his cheekbones were prominent and his nose very slightly hooked, giving strength and character to a face that, beneath an intense masculinity, looked exhausted. The body against hers was bone-hard. His head topped hers by six inches. She thought foolishly, he can't be the right man. This is Toronto in August and my nose is shiny and I'm late for work. He can't be.

The man straightened, pushing her away from him by resting his hands on her shoulders. He said formally, 'I'm terribly sorry. Did I hurt you?'

One small part of her brain decided immediately that he would be a good singer, for his voice had depth and resonance. The other major part seemed to be paralysed. She stammered, 'I-I was more worried about my guitar.'

'I didn't touch it, I assure you.'

She was gazing upwards, mesmerised. Although his manners were excellent and his voice without inflection, his hands were still clasping her shoulders, and she would have sworn that behind the guarded blue eyes he was battling with a strong emotion. She could not have guessed the nature of that emotion. But she was certain it was there. The surety of her knowledge rather frightened her; she had never thought she had inherited any of the prescience of her gypsy ancestress. Struggling to collect her wits, she managed to say, 'You didn't hurt me, no.' And because she was almost sure that he was the right man, that her quest was ended, she gave him a brilliant smile.

The light in the corridor shone down on her hair so that the tumbled curls were shot through with gold; her

eyes reflected the leaf-brown of a woodland pool. Her
cheeks were flushed and her lips a warm, soft curve. The
man's fingers tightened their hold; the emotion she had
been so sure of flared to life in the deep blue eyes.

From behind them the clipped voice of Mr Jodrey
said, 'Miss Gayle, you're late.'

Along with the peasant outfit, Mr Jodrey had
conferred upon Joss a working name, for he had
disapproved of Joss MacDougall as too countrified. So
she had become Jocelyn Gayle for the duration of the
summer, and on the rare occasions when male
customers overimbibed or gave her undue attention she
was glad enough of a pseudonym. Now, however, it
took her a moment to realise she was being spoken to.

The blue-eyed man dropped his hands and turned. Mr
Jodrey surveyed them both with impartial coldness,
then said to Joss, 'This is the second time in a week that
you have been late. As I am sure you are aware.'

It was confusing enough to meet the man of her
dreams in a hotel corridor. To have to deal with Mr
Jodrey on top of that seemed quite unfair. But the job
at the pub paid well and Joss needed the money. Trying
to inject the words with some sincerity, which was
difficult because she was simultaneously deciding that
she disliked Mr Jodrey's prissy little mouth, Joss said,
'I'm sorry, Mr Jodrey.'

Mr Jodrey drew himself up to his full five-feet nine,
which made him exactly Joss's height. 'Your contract is
to sing from five p.m. until nine p.m., Miss Gayle. *Five*
p.m. Not,' he consulted his wristwatch ostentatiously,
'five-ten.'

The blue-eyed man said calmly, 'I'm afraid I must
accept some of the blame. Miss Gayle and I bumped
into each other—quite literally—and we were concerned
about possible damage to her guitar.'

At the time when Mr Jodrey had spoken, Joss's guitar
had been dangling from her left hand, and she and the

tall stranger had been staring into each other's eyes. But
Mr Jodrey did not argue, for something about the blue-
eyed man bespoke authority. His beautifully tailored
grey pinstripe suit? His unconscious air of arrogance
that announced he was accustomed to the wielding of
power? Whatever it was, Mr Jodrey gave him an
obsequious bow.

Trying very hard not to laugh, Joss said with false
humility, 'I promise I won't be late again.'

'Very well,' said Mr Jodrey, not looking quite as
obsequious as he transferred his attention to Joss. 'But
kindly proceed to the bar immediately, Miss Gayle.'

Joss's jaw dropped. How could she leave? She did not
know the blue-eyed man's name or where he was from
or whether he was a guest at the hotel. She might never
see him again. Disconcerting enough that she had met
him in Toronto and not in the orchard. Quite impossible
that she should lose him as soon as she had found him.
She looked up at him, blurted, 'Are you coming to hear
me sing?' and heard Mr Jodrey's hiss of indrawn
breath; Mr Jodrey did not approve of staff associating
with guests.

The stranger—although Joss had difficulty thinking
of him as a stranger—must have heard this hiss as well.
He inclined his head and said urbanely, 'That will give
me great pleasure.'

She bestowed upon him a generous smile in which
relief was predominant, then with a hunted look at Mr
Jodrey raised her guitar in salute and scurried down the
hall towards the Red Lion. It took every ounce of her
will-power not to look back over her shoulder. Her
heart was thumping in her breast in a way that she knew
had nothing to do with her race to get from one job to
the next, and certainly nothing to do with pre-
performance nerves. Her brain was whirling. Her knees
were weak and her hands, oddly, ice-cold. It seemed a
peculiar combination of physical symptoms to have

resulted from a chance meeting. Nor did it even resemble the state of mind Joss had always imagined for herself in the orchard. There she had smiled dreamily at the faceless man and had made a number of witty and provocative remarks before being enfolded in his embrace. Now, as she entered the dimly lit bar, she remembered the lean, hard body with which she had collided and shivered inwardly.

Because the Swansea billed itself as a family hotel, the Red Lion featured Jocelyn Gayle singing folk songs early in the evening, followed by either a pianist or a small band for dancing. The bar itself was modelled on an old English pub, with deep, comfortable leather chairs and rather a lot of highly polished brass. The walls were panelled in oak and decorated with reproductions of old inn signs. Joss's stool was on a little raised dais. She perched herself on the stool, arranged her skirts, and began to tune her guitar. The blue-eyed man had not yet arrived.

When she began to play, her fingers felt slow and awkward and her throat was tight. She sang 'Jeanie with the Light Brown Hair' and a couple of leisurely Irish ballads to warm up her voice, acknowledged the discreet rattle of applause, then launched into a medley of Beatles' songs. Her audience consisted of men in business suits, a group of women much more interested in the contents of their shopping bags than in her, a honeymoon couple holding hands and paying her no attention whatsoever, and a sprinkling of tourists who had supplied the applause. She had sung to far less attentive audiences; indeed sometimes sang for her own benefit alone. She settled in, feeling her voice begin to fill out and relax. She loved to sing, deriving considerable amusement from being paid to do something that she so enjoyed.

She was half-way through 'Streets of London', a song that always made her wish she was Cleo Laine, when a tall man in a grey suit walked into the bar, looked around with a self-possession she could not have matched and sat down at the table nearest to her. By the time he had adjusted the chair so that he was facing her, the waitress was at his side; he was that kind of man, thought Joss, wishing even more strongly than usual that she was Cleo Laine. After he had ordered a drink he sat back, resting his elbows on the arms of the chair, his hands making a steeple. His eyes were fastened on her.

Miraculously she did not forget the words of the song, her fingers automatically plucking the strings on her guitar. He's here, her brain whispered. He's here, sitting twenty feet away from you. Sing, Joss. Sing your heart out.

So she did sing, and it seemed as though all the words were vested with a special magic, the pathos of the old man with yesterday's newspapers and the old woman whose clothes were in rags. The chattering women with the shopping bags glanced her way; the noisier group of tourists, in the far corner, were swaying to the music. But Joss was not singing to them. With gathering confidence she was singing to the man who was watching her so intently. When the waitress had brought his drink he had kept an open bill. He's going to be here for a while, Joss thought exultantly. He's not going to leave after just one drink.

But then she came to the part of the song about loneliness and with her heightened sensitivity saw how his eyes dropped and his hand encircled the glass so tightly that his knuckles were white. So, despite his air of arrogance, all was not right with his world, she thought slowly. He must be lonely sometimes, this handsome stranger; for him the sun did not always shine. It was a strange conclusion to reach in a crowded city bar.

He did not look up again until she had come to the

end of the song and the genuine burst of applause had died down. Something more cheerful, she decided quickly, and chose an old Welsh ballad about a beautiful young girl whose eyes tended to wander from her dutiful fiancé to the village ne'er-do-well. The chorus was catchy and easily learned. The tourists joined in, and even the honeymoon couple clapped in rhythm to the music. The ending had a surprise twist. The blue-eyed man smiled, and Joss's heart fluttered in her breast.

She did not allow the momentum to die down. In half an hour, when Mr Jodrey made one of his seemingly casual perambulations of the bar, she had the entire place in the palm of her hand. She knew it. He knew it, too. She gave him a wide-eyed, innocent smile, and saw that the man in the grey suit was laughing at her. She grinned at him impudently. He likes me, she thought dizzily. And he's got a sense of humour. The man in the orchard had been too ethereal to have had anything as earthy as a sense of humour.

At seven o'clock she announced to her audience that after the next song she would be taking a short break; this was a requirement in her contract. In the middle of the song the group of tourists in the far corner got up to leave. The two women were grey-haired and plump, and could have come from any of the farms around Alderney; one of the men had drunk more than was good for him, although he was a cheerful drunk rather than a morose one, singing to himself as he lurched between the seats, leaning over the honeymoon couple to whisper something, then roaring with laughter. His wife, in the green cotton dress, was plainly mortified by his behaviour. Joss added another verse to the song, hoping to distract attention from them to herself.

'Come along, Tom,' she heard the wife say. 'Do come along. You're making a fool of yourself.'

'Gotta tip the singer,' Tom boomed. 'Let go now,

Millie. I'll leave when I'm good and ready.'

Millie, unhappily, let go. Tom bumped against the blue-eyed man's chair, said with a *bonhomie* impervious to the chill in those eyes, 'Sorry, friend. Great little singer, eh? Always been partial to blondes, I have.' Without waiting for a reply he pulled out a wad of bank notes from the back pocket of his trousers, peeled off a ten-dollar bill and shoved the rest of the money into his pocket.

Hoping to ward off an embarrassing scene, Joss finished the song, acknowledged the applause and said into the microphone, 'Thank you, ladies and gentlemen. I'll be back in ten minutes.' However, just as she stood up, shaking out her skirts, Tom negotiated the step on to the dais. Narrowly missing the microphone stand, he pushed the ten-dollar bill into the neckline of her blouse, his watch strap scraping her skin, and said thickly, 'Give us a kiss. Great little singer.'

The microphone was turned on; the whole room must have heard Tom's request. Her eyes glittering, Joss twisted away from him. But Tom, however drunk, was a customer, and the customer, according to Mr Jodrey, was always right. Therefore she must not tell Tom what he could do with his ten-dollar bill. Nor must she poke him in the nose. What she must do was get out of the pub without causing a ruckus.

The blue-eyed man stepped neatly between her and Tom. He took her by the elbow and said calmly, 'Please allow me to escort you.'

His grip was like a steel clamp; she would have had difficulty refusing. Already he was propelling her across the little stage, leaving poor Tom, no doubt open-mouthed, with only the microphone for company. Holding her head high, Joss walked swiftly between the tables and past the bar. Millie and her two companions were standing by the door. Joss forcibly slowed her steps, smiled directly into Mille's humiliated grey eyes and said, 'Thank you for clapping. I'm glad you enjoyed the singing.' Then she was being hustled through the door, down the corridor, and around the corner where she had first met her escort.

He brought her round to face him; his hold was not overly gentle. 'Does that kind of thing happen often?' he demanded.

Joss would not have had to be very observant to see that he was furious. 'Not often, no,' she said, both puzzled and flattered by his anger.

'So where was Mr Jodrey when you needed him?'

'If there's a real problem, either the bartender or one of the bellboys comes to my rescue . . . I don't understand why you're so angry—and you're hurting my elbow.'

Her words seemed to bring him back to himself. He dropped her elbow, wiping all expression from his face. 'I'm sorry,' he said.

'Oh, please,' Joss said in laughing dismay. 'Now I've made you angrier.' He did not smile back. He reminded her very strongly of the image she had had of Heathcliff when she was fifteen: brooding, enigmatic and disturbingly masculine. Trying to slow her heart-rate, which seemed to react to him quite indiscriminately, Joss leaned her guitar against the wall, then flicked the ten-dollar bill out of the neckline of her blouse, holding the money away from her rather as if it were a particularly loathsome spider. Then she glanced up at her companion; he did not look quite as grim. Encouraged, she said with great sincerity, 'Thank you for rescuing me. You got me out of a very awkward situation.'

'I couldn't have you hitting a customer,' he replied imperturbably.

She gave a delighted little chuckle. 'You could tell that I was tempted, could you?'

'The light of battle was in your eyes. But I'm quite

sure your boss would rank assault as a far more heinous crime than unpunctuality.'

'All crimes are heinous to Mr Jodrey. But assault would be a little more heinous,' Joss admitted, then heard herself add, 'I grew up with four brothers who often considered a good fight the easiest way to solve a problem.'

'In my experience it usually adds to the problem.'

'Certainly Tom might not have taken kindly to a clout on the nose,' she said gravely.

'And what will you do with the ten dollars?'

She wrinkled her nose. 'If I were rich I'd probably burn it, or tear it into shreds and throw them to the four winds. As I'm not, I'll put it in my bank account.' She looked at him through her lashes, her eyes alive with mischief. 'Another grand gesture down the drain.'

She had finally made him smile. But he smiled stiffly, as if he were not quite used to doing it, Joss thought, and remembered her intuitive sense that at some level he was quite dreadfully lonely. Close up his face was gaunt, his eyes of so burning a blue that they seemed to have drawn all the colour from the surrounding features. He looked like an over-trained racehorse, she decided thoughtfully, driven beyond his capabilities.

Under her scrutiny his eyes had veiled themselves. He said, 'And where did you grow up with your four brothers, Jocelyn Gayle?'

'Joss,' she said quickly. 'Please call me Joss. I grew up in Nova Scotia—and you haven't told me your name.'

'Niall.' He spelled it. 'I have a great objection to being called Neil with an e.'

He had not volunteered his last name. She had about five minutes of her break left in which to discover it. 'Your name sounds Irish,' she ventured. He gave such a non-committal nod that she abandoned subtlety. 'You haven't told me your last name.'

He raised one eyebrow. 'Diamond?'

'I'm sure you can sing, but I'm equally sure you're not Neil Diamond. Besides, he had an e in his name.'

'Let's use it anyway.'

Joss frowned. 'If you don't want to tell me your last name, just say so.'

'I don't.'

She had not expected such an unequivocal reply. 'Why are you being so mysterious?'

'Would you prefer me to be stuffing ten-dollar bills down your blouse?'

She flushed. 'I'd hate that. As you know.'

'So what's a nice girl like you doing singing in a Toronto bar?'

'Trying to keep body and soul together,' Joss said as lightly as she could, not liking the turn of the conversation, but quite unable to alter it to anything approaching her imaginary conversations in the orchard. '*I* could ask why a man as uptight as you is talking to a woman who sings in a bar. Couldn't I?'

'I'm asking myself exactly the same question.'

'Oh, are you?' Joss raised her chin and wondered if she would ever be able to enjoy the sight of apple blossoms again. 'Please don't let me keep you!'

'Are you by chance accusing me of being a snob?'

'You certainly sound like one.'

He ran his fingers through his hair in exasperation. 'Well, I'm not. You could be a garbage collector or a lady-in-waiting to the Queen—I couldn't care less.'

Oddly enough, she believed him. 'I'm neither one. I grew up on a farm, this is my first time in a big city, and I hate it,' she announced. She added astutely, 'So it's not my occupation that bothers you—it's your own behaviour.'

Again Joss saw that brief smile that seemed to hurt something deep within him. 'Very clever. You certainly say what's on your mind.'

'Something else my brothers taught me.' She decided to live up to her reputation. 'Are you going back to the bar after my break?'

During the long moment Niall regarded her unsmilingly, Joss had time to think that by now the man in the orchard would have clasped her to his bosom and rained kisses on her lips. She was sure the mysterious Niall was not going to clasp her to his bosom. Nor did he. He said flatly, 'Yes.'

She had not realised how frightened she was of his reply until after he had made it. She let out her breath in a tiny sigh. 'I have the feeling that everything you say means at least five other things besides.'

'You're not far wrong.'

She had known she was not. She said, 'I have go to back—my break's just about over.'

'Tom marked your skin.'

Surprised, Joss glanced down. Just above the embroidered ruffle of her blouse was a shallow graze left by Tom's watch strap. 'It's nothing,' she mumbled, and like someone under a spell watched Niall's finger trace the blemish on her flesh. His touch was like a lick of fire. It's just as well he hasn't put his arms around me, she thought wildly. I'd have melted on the spot. 'I have to go,' she stammered. 'I mustn't be late again.'

'Look at me, Joss.'

Knowing her cheeks were scarlet and her eyes no doubt as wild as her thoughts, she obeyed. Niall said harshly, 'Are you as you seem, Jocelyn Gayle?'

'I-I don't understand.'

'You seem so real—I feel as thought I know a great deal about you just by having watched you. You don't put up with any nonsense from men like Tom, yet you were kind enough to take a minute to talk to his wife. You sing with a deep feeling for the music. And you're so very beautiful.'

The faceless man in the orchard vanished for ever. Joss was left with a tall stanger whose burning blue eyes seemed to see right through her. 'I'm nothing out of the ordinary,' she said with faint desperation. 'I grew up on a farm. I've always loved to sing. I'm trying to make my way in the world. That's all.'

'You have no idea how rare a virtue kindness is,' Niall responded shortly. 'Disinterested kindness. Don't ever lose it.'

She should be back in the Red Lion, perched on her stool, singing for the guests. But she could not leave. Not yet. 'The reverse of your statement isn't true—I feel as though I know nothing about you,' she said. 'Not even your name.'

'You know I couldn't stand by and watch Tom maul you—you know that much.'

'Why not?'

He stirred restlessly under her scrutiny. 'Let's skip that question.'

'You couldn't have been jealous . . .'

'If you say not.'

'You're playing with me!' she burst out. 'Like a cat with a mouse. I hate games, Mr Niall Whatever-your-name-is.'

'Then stay away from me,' he answered with deadly calm. 'Because that's the only way I can play it.'

She hesitated. 'Is that why you brought me out here?' she asked painfully. 'To tell me that?'

'Yes,' he said sombrely. 'Yes, I suppose you could say that's why.'

Her fantasy collapsed like a punctured balloon; the man who should have been her soulmate would not even tell her his last name. Joss seized her guitar with less than her usual care, whirled, and fled down the corridor. She felt sick at heart. She had always envisaged the attraction between herself and her imaginary love as mutual. They would come face to face and in a single perfect moment they would recognise each other once and for all. No misunderstandings. No conflict. Just the warm glow of the noonday sun that casts no shadows . . .

There was no sign of Mr Jodrey in the pub. Joss said a rather breathless good evening into the microphone, tuned her guitar and began to sing some Broadway hits that she knew from experience would be popular. 'The Surrey with the Fringe on Top' brought Niall back into the bar. Her voice wavered on a high note, for after his words in the corridor she had been afraid he would not reappear. The knot in her breast loosened; so he was a man who kept his promises. With more gusto she sang about corn as high as an elephant's eye and about the perils and delights of Kansas City. The audience was more mellow now, the waitresses busier, the smoke thicker. She announced she was open for requests and, her voice warm and true, sang 'Don't Cry for Me, Argentina'. Niall was staring down at the tabletop, his face inscrutable. But at least he was there, Joss thought, her fingers caressing the strings.

The requests trickled in. Joss had learned ballads and folk songs from her mother, war tunes and big band songs from her father, and more recent hits on her own; her versatility had been partly responsible for getting her the job. She enjoyed the challenge of trying to grant people's wishes, and was only rarely stumped. But at a quarter to nine a little white-haired lady in an old-fashioned taffeta dres, who had been tossing back Martinis as if they were water, marched firmly up to the dais and requested a Celtic song that Joss had never heard of. She listened intently as the old lady went through the first verse in a cracked voice, her diamond-encrusted fingers tapping out the melody. Joss had always been quick to pick up new tunes and within five minutes had produced a reasonable facsimile of the song. She glanced over at Niall's table to see if he had been amused by her improvisations.

He was not there. His glass was drained. A tidy pile of notes lay on top of his bill.

Her fingers struck a discord. Frantically her eyes searched the room, but he was nowhere to be seen.

Said the little old lady, 'That was sweet of you, dear. Do you know "The Mountains of Moran"?'

Joss did. She got through it somehow, then sang 'The Whistling Gypsy' with less than her usual verve. Niall msut be waiting for her outside, she thought numbly as she smiled and sang and played. He did not want to get her into trouble with Mr Jodrey. So he had left a little early and would be waiting for her in the lobby or on the pavement in front of the hotel.

At nine sharp she swept the last resounding chord from her guitar, smiled, bowed, said her thanks into the microphone and threaded her way between the tables. Niall was not in the hall outside the Red Lion, nor was he in the corridor. Of course not, she told herself. That was still Mr Jodrey's territory. Niall was too discreet to wait for her there.

She stripped off her peasant outfit in the staff room, hung it up, and replaced her guitar in the locker. Anxious though she was, she took a moment to repair her make-up and run a brush through her hair. There was a hectic patch of colour on each cheek; her eyes were very bright. Aware that at some deep level she was breathing a frenzied prayer over and over again, Joss snapped the padlock on her locker and left the room.

The lobby with its gilt chandeliers and peach and green carpets was almost deserted. Six staff members. Twelve guests. No Niall. The doorman, red-faced and jolly in his brass-buttoned uniform, winked at her and said jovially, 'All through, Joss? Must be nice.'

She gave him a distracted smile. 'Russell, you haven't seen a tall man in a grey suit in the last few minutes, have you?'

'That's kind of like going to the library and asking for the book with the red cover,' Russell replied; he liked to tease the pretty young women on staff.

'Very tall, very good-looking, dark hair, blue eyes,' she said rapidly.

'About quarter to nine a man answering to that description got me to hail a cab. Tipped me two dollars, he did.'

Her face fell. 'Did you hear where he was going?'

Russell shook his head, regarding her inquisitively. 'Friend of yours?'

Her shoulders were drooping. Not looking at him, she muttered, 'I don't know.'

'Never seen you go after a man before.'

That was because she never had. She said urgently, 'Russell, if you see him again, will you try and find out his name for me? His first name's Niall. That's all I know.'

'Looked like kind of a tough customer to me. Things on his mind, I'd say. More important things than women.'

'Don't be a chauvinist,' she said absently, peering down the length of the street. Between the tall office buildings of downtown Toronto the sky was shrouded in darkness; the cars had their headlights on, and the traffic lights at the corner flashed their repetitive message of 'Stop, Caution, Go'. Too late for caution, she thought unhappily. Four hours too late. And she had nowhere to go but to the apartment.

Joss shared an apartment with an old schoolfriend, Magda Trevanian, who was also a singer and who had found Joss the job at the Red Lion. Magda, who had flamboyant red hair and a gorgeous body, sang with a band in a nightclub and never got home before two in the morning; consequently she was usually asleep when Joss left for the bookshop in the mornings, and sometimes a week would pass without them seeing each other. Now, as Joss trudged towards the subway station, she was glad the apartment would be empty. She did not want to have to describe an encounter that had ended so inconclusively, whose emotional overtones had been so intense. Instense for herself, she added as she tramped down the stone steps. Had she been wrong to sense that Niall had, in his own way, been as affected by the encounter as she? Wishful thinking? An extension of her romantic daydream? After all, if he had been affected, why had he disappeared? The normal response would have been to ask her for a date.

She showed her subway pass to the ticket agent and pushed through the turnstile. The platform was crowded, and almost immediately one of the blunt-nosed trains racketed out of the tunnel and hissed to a halt along the platform. Joss stepped aboard and stood near the sliding doors. Niall hadn't asked her for a date because he was married.

Come off it, she told herself firmly. Lots of married men pick up girls in bars. Certainly they don't make any secret of their last names. Anyway, he didn't look married.

Nor had he. He had looked, instead, very much a loner. Joss braced herself as the brakes squealed and the train juddered to a halt at the next station. Maybe he was unhappily married, she thought, and rather than deceive her he had simply left.

By the time she had travelled for two more station stops and had climbed the steps to the street again, night had fallen. She walked fast and purposely along the two blocks to the apartment, located on a narrow side street in an old Victorian house that in five years would no doubt be knocked down to make way for another of the box-like condominiums that dotted the neighbourhood; in the meantime the rent was affordable.

Magda was by nature untidy. Three shopping bags had been dumped on the faded old chesterfield,

Magda's jogging outfit lay in an exhausted heap on the floor and a pile of books had been thrown on the bamboo table that served as desk, eating place and sewing bench. Magda's cat, a fat, self-centred tortoiseshell named Nasturtium, took up the only other chair in the room. Joss had learned to live with Magda's untidiness for the sake of her cooking; Magda could take the most unpromising leftovers and transform them into dishes that would not have disgraced a five-star restaurant. But although Joss now drank some cream of spinach soup that had been left on the stove and consumed two fluffy braided rolls, she could scarcely have said what she was eating. Aimlessly she pushed her spoon around the bottom of the bowl. She had too much pride to phone her mother and explain that the right man had been the wrong man; and she was too tired, physically and mentally, to analyse why she had responded with such instinctive force to a complete stranger. Very carefully trying not to think at all, she washed the dishes, swept the kitchen floor, had a shower and went to bed. Nasturtium jumped up on the bed with her; her purr, the most energetic part of her personality, was obscurely comforting. Joss closed her eyes tightly and whisked herself from the stuffy apartment in Toronto to the beach that lay five miles from the farm, where the waves cavorted on the sand and the gulls, drenched in sunlight, wheeled in slow circles overhead. She was home, home where she belonged . . . and where the right man was still an unrealised dream in the orchard.

CHAPTER TWO

JOSS only worked for four hours at the bookshop on Thurdays, from ten until two; this was an arrangement that suited her well, enabling her to do household chores, banking and grocery shopping. She had woken that morning in a militantly rational mood, determined to put the mysterious blue-eyed Niall in his proper place. Because she was homesick she was vulnerable. Because she was vulnerable she had chosen to interpret a chance meeting with a stranger as a fulfilment of a youthful fantasy. The sooner she forgot him, the better. She was crazy to believe he was of lasting significance in her life.

Because she did not have to leave the apartment until nine-thirty, she was still home when the mail was delivered. There was a business letter addressed to her from the research laboratory where she had worked for the past two summers and would have been working this summer had not government cutbacks obliterated half of the junior positions. She opened the letter. The director had received a grant and was offering Joss a full-time job starting in October as a research assistant level II.

She put the letter on the table, pouring herself another cup of tea. When she had graduated last spring with an honours degree she had applied to three medical schools and had been accepted at Dalhousie in Halifax and the University of Western Ontario, which was a couple of hours from Toronto. Two acceptances had been good for her ego. But she had also been pulled in another direction. Her parents were no longer young and had never been rich, and Joss had very much wanted to get a job and be in the position to give them some of the things they had had to do without to raise their seven children. Even though Joss had always had summer jobs and had been largely self-supporting throughout university, her mother had been apt to slip twenty dollars into each of her letters, or to send generous packages including everything from home-made cookies to toothpaste. Joss would now like to be able to return those favours. If she went to medical school she faced another six years of scrimping for every penny.

She folded up the letter and put it in her purse, her hazel eyes reflective. She would have to make a decision soon, for the deadline for the final despoit for medical school was in ten days' time. If she accepted the job offer she would be home in Nova Scotia. She could visit the farm at weekends. With a sharp pang of longing she realised just how badly she missed her family. Maybe she would take the job, forget about medical school.

She left the apartment, spent a productive four hours organising the remaindered books on the long tables on the second floor of the bookshop, ran several errands and arrived at the Swansea with half an hour to spare. It took all her self-control to keep a steady pace as she rounded the corner where she had met Niall, but managed to do so. When she passed Mr Jodrey just outside the staff room she gave him a rather smug smile; they both knew she was almost never this early.

Joss took her time getting changed, tuned her guitar in the staff room, and determinedly kept her thoughts on the job offer and the very satisfactory state of her bank account. At seven minutes to five she walked sedately down the corridor to the Red Lion. Her father would be proud of her; her father was the rational member of the family.

The bar in the Red Lion, with its racks of shining

glasses and array of bottles, was on the right, just inside the entrance to the pub. The counter was oval-shaped with a brass rail and tall oak stools; a blue-eyed man was seated on the stool nearest the entrance.

Joss stopped dead, nearly dropping her guitar. She said flatly, 'What are *you* doing here?'

Today Niall was wearing casual white cotton trousers and a short-sleeved red shirt. Lounging against the bar, he gave her an unpleasant smile and indicated the two glasses at his elbow, the nearer one almost empty, the other full. 'Getting drunk,' he said.

She was suddenly furious, far angrier than she had been with Tom the day before, angrier than she could ever remember being. The gold flecks in her eyes like tiny sparks, she said with dangerous quietness, 'Still playing your little games, aren't you?'

He tipped back his head and drained the contents of the nearer glass. His thoat was strongly muscled and deeply tanned; she could see the dark tangle of body hair in the open neckline of his shirt, and somehow that stoked her rage. Taking his time, Niall replaced the empty glass on the counter and picked up the full one. 'That's right,' he said. 'Cheers.'

'Why don't you just leave?' she seethed. 'Right now.'

'Tch, tch, Jocelyn Gayle,' he said mockingly. 'Remember Mr Jodrey—the customer's always right. Particularly a customer who's spending as much money as I am today.'

'Why are you *doing* this?'

'It's a free country.' Niall took a long pull at the new drink.

He was not slurring his words and his movements were perfectly controlled; yet she sensed in him an anger that more than matched her own. She did not care. She wanted to scream at him at the top of her lungs and drum her heels on the floor. Keeping the bartender and Mr Jodrey in mind, she muttered ferociously, 'I want you to go away and leave me alone.'

'I didn't start this conversation. You did.' He added with great interest, 'You look like a jungle cat when you're angry. Those tawny eyes and that mane of hair. Am I allowed to buy you a drink? To congratulate you on being early for work?'

'No!'

He raised one brow. 'No, thank you?' he murmured.

She felt as frustrated as she had years ago on the rare occasions when her four brothers had ganged up on her, taunting her for being only a girl. No matter how loudly she had yelled at them or how hard she had beaten her pudgy fists against their chests, she had never been able to make any impression on them. Matters were not helped now when Niall said silkily, 'Don't try and bash me with your guitar, Jocelyn Gayle. I'm not Tom.'

Very much aware of the lean, powerful body under the casual summer clothes, a body which in no way resembled Tom's, Joss said with great venom, if no particular originality, 'I wouldn't think of it—I value my guitar.'

He had the audacity to laugh. 'Oh, dear. That does put me in my place. By the way, hadn't you better start singing? It's five o'clock.'

Despite her fondness for the memory of Great-Aunt Lucy, it would have given Joss tremendous satisfaction to have brought the guitar down on Niall's head. 'Just don't bother me between now and nine o'clock,' she said tautly. 'Do you hear me?'

'I've never been accused of deafness,' Niall said blandly. 'But if I might make a suggestion, I'd avoid "Streets of London" if I were you. Cleo Laine is the only woman who should sing that song.'

Unfortunately Joss agreed with him. 'I don't have the time to stand here trading insults with you,' she choked.

'No, you don't. Two minutes after five.'

Not trusting herself to say another word, Joss pivoted

and stalked past the bar to the dais. Someone had shifted her stool and the microphone nearer to the tables. Not bothering to move them, she sat down in a swirl of skirts, adjusted the angle of the microphone and said into it with a vivacity fuelled by anger, 'Good afternoon, ladies and gentlemen. My name is Jocelyn Gayle and I'm here to sing for your pleasure from now until nine o'clock this evening. Please feel free to request any songs you would like . . . and please enjoy.'

With a wild clash of chords she threw herself into 'The Whistling Gypsy', a song she usually saved for later in her show when the audience had warmed up. She followed it by several extremely energetic Israeli folk songs. In the final verse of the last song a tall man in a red shirt sauntered between the tables and stretched out in a chair just to her right. His foot was within six inches of her green ruffled skirt.

Joss was in good voice and the adrenalin was still coursing through her veins. She gave the man a vivid smile, running her fingers through her hair in a deliberately seductive gesture, and said into the microphone, 'I've had a request from the gentleman to my right. Cleo Laine's version of "Cavatina", which you may also know as "He Was So Beautiful".'

With exquisite sensibility she played the first slow arpeggio. She sang, looking directly into Niall's eyes. She could tell she had taken him by surprise. More than surprise: he looked stunned. Her voice caressed the notes, giving each its due, as she held his gaze.

But then with a pang at her heart Joss remembered the orchard and the beautiful man who had been waiting for her there in the springtime, and in spite of herself the poignancy of the song overcame her anger. When she sang of shared moments and lingering feelings she had to look away, and her audience was absolutely silent as she ended the song.

In rare tribute there was an instant of quiet before the people in the pub began to clap. Joss bowed her head, fighting back tears, knowing her trick had backfired on her. She should have rehearsed the words in her head before she began to sing; had she done so, she would never have chosen that song.

' "Danny Boy"!' someone shouted from the back of the room.

Another surefire tearjerker, she thought wryly, and as the first chord rippled from her guitar she sneaked a glance through her lashes at Niall. He was staring full at her, his face a grim, frozen mask. Hastily she looked away, her blood pounding in her veins. Niall had been no more indifferent to that song than she had been.

From 'Danny Boy' she moved to the safer terrain of 'An English Country Garden'; enough emotion for one night. Perhaps because it was Thursday and near the end of the week her audience was very receptive, so that for minutes at a time Joss was able to ignore the man on her right, who was still steadily drinking, still seemingly unaffected by what he was drinking. She did not even look at him when she left the pub for her break; he was sitting at the same table when she returned and, as she sat down, winked at her sardonically.

She looked haughtily down her nose and then turned away, presenting him with her profile. She had a straight, decided nose and a firm chin. For her ears alone Niall drawled, 'I like a woman with spirit.'

Joss raised her chin perceptibly, sang a Caribbean fisherman's ballad and then a rather bawdy sea shanty that Great-Aunt Lucy would have enjoyed. The second half of the evening seemed to pass very quickly, and at nine o'clock when she announced into the microphone that her time was up Niall was still sitting at the chair nearest her. Had she consumed the amount of alcohol that he had, she would have been flat under the table; he, however, looked exactly as he had at five o'clock. Furthermore, he looked as though he had settled in for the night. Because one of Mr Jodrey's strictest rules was that she not fraternise with the guests, Joss could not do what she wanted to, which was sit down at his table and talk to him. They wouldn't even have to talk, she thought helplessly. Just to be with him would be enough. So much for rationality.

Her face showing none of the turmoil of her thoughts, she gathered up her guitar and left the dais without a backwards look. A middle-aged couple sitting near the entranceway signalled her over; they were from Ireland, and, after telling her how much they had enjoyed her singing, began discussing the words to 'The Maid With the Nut-Brown Hair'. At any other time Joss would have been delighted to learn a new verse to a song that she loved; now, however, all she wanted to do was escape from the Red Lion.

She did finally make her escape, and changed into her street clothes in the staff room. She decided to leave the hotel via the lobby again, on the off-chance that Niall might be there. He was not. Gripping the strap of her shoulderbag she turned on her heel, marched in the door of the Red Lion, and walked past the bar. The seat beside the dais was empty.

She blinked and looked again. Niall had quite definitely gone.

The bartender was a young man called Claude Montaigne who had only been working at the Red Lion for a couple of weeks. Joss said hurriedly, 'Claude, did the man in the red shirt leave?'

'He paid 'is bill and left right after you.' Claude rolled his eyes. 'A big bill, a big tip. 'E can come back any time.'

'Thanks.' Forgetting decorum, Joss ran across the lobby and pushed against the swing door. Then she

stopped in dismay. It was pouring with rain. She had a
vague recollection that the weather report that morning
had mentioned rain, but she had been too busy
considering her job offer to pay much attention. She
had not bothered with a raincoat or an umbrella.

Russell was on duty outside, holding a huge umbrella
over some newly arrived guests. He grinned at Joss and
indicated the street running west. 'He went thataway,'
he called.

She knew Russell was referring to Niall. She drew a
deep breath and plunged out into the rain; fortunately
her cotton skirt and knit top were washable. As was the
rest of her, she thought ruefully as the cool drops pelted
her face and trickled down her neck.

The hotel took up the rest of the block. Joss ran to the
corner, her sandals slapping against the wet pavement,
and looked to her left and then to her right. A man in a
red shirt was stationed beyond the next set of traffic
lights, trying to flag down a taxi.

Clutching her bag she ran after him, and had her
father appeared in front of her and asked what she was
doing she could not have produced a sensible answer.
She reached the lights; she was perhaps forty feet from
Niall. A yellow cab had pulled up on the opposite side
of the street from him.

The walk signal flashed. Joss stepped off the
pavement.

To her right a car horn blared. Instinctively she
retreated, pushing her wet hair out of her eyes. A
souped-up jalopy with only one headlight was racing
towards her. The traffic light was red; instead of
stopping, the jalopy took the corner in a squeal of tyres.
Niall had already checked to see if there was anything
coming. As if everything was happening in slow motion,
Joss saw him step off the kerb into the path of the the
the oncoming car.

She screamed his name. *'Niall!* Niall, stop!' Then

she began to run, faster than she had ever run in her life.

His head had swivelled at the sound of her voice. He saw the car immediately and leaped backwards on to the pavement. The jalopy blasted its horn again and careened past him; the driver had not even touched the brakes.

Joss stumbled to a halt, grabbing at a newspaper stand for support, gasping for breath. The cab driver, who belonged to a group of people normally unshockable, had rolled down his window and was watching the retreating jalopy, shaking his head. Niall said sharply, 'Joss! Are you all right?'

Slowly she straightened. As a fifteen-year-old she had been a devotee of gothic novels; the hearts of their delicate white-clad heroines had been wont to skip beats with distressing frequency. But Joss had never known it could actually happen. She took a couple of steps towards Niall, amazed that all her joints seemed to be functioning and that she could put one foot in front of the other. 'I'm fine,' she said more or less truthfully. 'What about yourself?'

His hair was stuck to his skull and his shirt plastered to his body; he looked lean and dangerous, and somehow his next question came as no surprise. 'What the hell are you doing here?' he demanded.

The cabbie yelled, 'Hey! You two wanna go someplace?'

Over his shoulder Niall called, 'Pull over and start your meter. I'll be with you in a second.' Then he looked back at Joss. 'I asked you a question.'

Now that she had stopped running, her wet clothes were sticking to her body, making her shiver. 'I was following you,' she said.

'How flattering,' Niall sneered. 'You should have saved yourself the trouble.' But as he spoke he swayed a little on his feet, and for the first time Joss

remembered the amount of alcohol he had consumed.
She closed the gap between them, reached out one hand
and rested it on his wrist. The contact shuddered
through her body. 'Niall, why don't we go somewhere
where we can get out of the rain and have a cup of
coffee? Maybe even something to eat.'

He pulled his arm free. 'No.'

'Mister,' the cab driver shouted, 'I can earn more on
a fare than sittin' here all night. You comin'?'

'No, he's not,' Joss yelled back.

'Yes, I am,' Niall snapped.

'You can't just leave me here!'

'I didn't ask you to follow me.'

'Then why did you come to the bar tonight?' she
blazed.

The cabbie said in a loud voice, spacing each word,
'This is your last chance, you guys.'

'Because I'm a fool,' Niall said savagely. 'A
goddamned fool.' Turning his back on her, he crossed
the street in a few long strides, opened the back door of
the cab and climbed in, then slammed the door shut; the
cab's registration number was painted on the side.

'Ain't she comin', too?' the driver demanded. From
her stance on the pavement Joss could see that he was
young, with curly black hair and a broken nose.
Presumably Niall answered in the negative, because the
young man said, more loudly, 'She saved your life,
fella! That car wasn't stoppin' for nobody.'

The scene had all the elements of farce; chivalry was
found in strange guises. But through the driving rain
Joss saw Niall lean forward, mouthing words she could
not hear. The cabbie gave a philosophical shrug and
called out to Joss, 'Sorry, honey. But a fare's a fare.
There'll be another cab along in a couple of minutes.' In
a swish of water he drove away.

Hugging her bag, Joss stood still by the news-stand.
In the movies she would now hail another taxi, cry,

'Follow that car!' and trace Niall to his destination. They would have a dramatic shouting match in the foyer of his apartment building and then he would take her in his arms and kiss her passionately. Her hair, of course, would not be clinging to her face like wet seaweed.

She scowled into the rain. Had ten taxis appeared she would not have asked one of them to follow Niall, for although outwardly she was shivering, inwardly she was boiling with rage. The cabbie was right. She *had* saved Niall's life. But he had not seen fit to thank her. Oh, no! He had preferred to insult her and reject her and leave her standing in the rain. On a poorly lit side street, she noticed with a further upsurge of rage. Anyone more removed from her lover in the orchard could not be imagined. *He* would not have left her standing in the rain.

Right, she thought ironically, beginning to trudge back the way she had come; there was no point in hurrying, for she was as wet as she could possibly get. The man in the orchard would have thrown a velvet cloak around her shoulders, lifted her on the back of his milk-white steed and carried her off into the sunset. The cloak would have been trimmed with ermine.

She walked a little slower, hunching her shoulders, staring down at her sandals, whose straps were leaving ugly brown stains on her bare feet. I don't want a velvet cloak, she thought with painful honesty. Or a white stallion. All I want is a little common courtesy, and an explanation why Niall had turned up at the Red Lion for the second night in a row. The cloak and the steed were the trappings of romance. What she wanted was the real person. Niall, the man.

But Niall had chosen not to give her that. He had spoken to her in riddles, he had stared at her as if he hungered for her with all his soul, and then, twice, he had vanished.

She reached the traffic lights, carefully looked in all four directions, then crossed the street, heading for the subway station. She must forget about him, she adjured herself. He was no good for her. He was rude and full of anger. Secretive. Arrogant. Overbearing. Her steps quickened. The cab driver had shown her more consideration than Niall had. For reasons she could not begin to understand, Niall was a bitter, twisted man, and for her to believe even for a moment that he was the right man for her was lunacy. The right man existed, she was still convinced of that; but she had yet to meet him.

To Joss's surprise, when she was sitting at the bamboo table the next morning sipping a cup of coffee and reading the headlines, Magda opened her bedroom door and propped herself in the doorway. Magda had a mop of glorious red hair, a sexy body and come-hither green eyes, all of which concealed a practical, no-nonsense personality and a kindness strongly tempered by common sense.

Said Joss blankly, 'What are you doing up so early?'

Magda glided into the room, looked at the heap of her own clothes on the chair as if wondering whose they were, dumped them on the floor and sat down. The tortoiseshell cat jumped into her lap, kneading the folds of Magda's fashionable striped nightshirt. 'Is that all you're having for breakfast?' Magda said severely.

'I had a piece of toast.'

'You'd starve to death if it wasn't for my cooking.'

'No, I wouldn't—I'd be five pounds lighter.' Joss grinned at her roommate. 'You didn't get out of bed at eight-thirty to ask me what I had for breakfast.'

'Charlie proposed to me yesterday afternoon.' Reflectively Magda stroked the cat, her green eyes shrewd. 'I think I'll accept.'

Charlie was five-feet-ten, as thin as a rail, and quite frighteningly intelligent. He called himself an inventor, supporting this so far unlucrative vocation by working as a night-watchman at a construction site, a job that he said gave him lots of time to think. Although his features were instantly forgettable and his physique nothing remarkable, he seemed quite unsurprised that a creature as gorgeous as Madga should spend all her free time with him.

Joss said drily, 'So would I be premature to congratulate you?'

Madga's full lips smiled provocatively. 'I believe you'd be quite safe.'

Joss got up, hugged her friend, a move not appreciated by Nasturtium, and said sincerely, 'I wish you both all the happiness in the world.'

'We'll probably get married in the autumn and move into Charlie's apartment.'

Charlie lived in the kind of apartment that landlords described as 'having possibilities'. Joss said dubiously, 'You won't have much money.'

'Not at first. But we will have,' Madga said calmly. 'I have faith in Charlie.'

Joss said impulsively, 'Magda, are you sure he's the right man for you?'

'Absolutely.'

'Did you know that right away?'

Magda tickled the cat's ears. 'He was different. So many of the men I meet at the club want to undress me within five minutes of meeting me. Whereas Charlie wanted to talk about the book I was reading. He didn't even kiss me until the fourth date, and then it was on the cheek.'

'So you didn't fall madly in love with him at first sight,' Joss said slowly.

'That only happens in books.' Magda tipped the cat on the floor. 'I'm going to brew some proper Colombian coffee—not that slop you're drinking. Want some?'

'Sure,' Joss said absently, wondering if Magda was right. Somethig had happened between herself and Niall, to that she would swear. But Niall had made it clear he did not want her, and she was dismayed that of all the men in the world her emotions had been touched by someone so unapproachable, so difficult, so angry. If she could only understand why he had such an effect on her, she might be better able to obliterate that effect. Because she was quite sure that after last night she would not see him again.

However, when Joss arrived at the side door of the Swansea Hotel at four-thirty that afternoon, a tall, blue-eyed man was waiting for her in the alleyway. He was wearing a trench coat over light grey trousers. Her footsteps slowed and she heard the bumpity-bump of her heart over the patter of rain on her umbrella. Happiness and anger warred within her; she remembered being left at the kerbside in the rain in the dark, put her nose in the air and reached for the door-handle.

Niall grabbed the sleeve of her raincoat. 'Don't go in—I've got to talk to you.'

Ineffectively she tried to pull her arm free. '*I* don't want to talk to *you*.'

'Please, Joss. I have to apologise. I behaved very badly last night.'

'You're so right. Let go of my arm.'

He dropped it instantly. She seized the door-handle and turned it, but Niall's foot was now wedged against the door. She said with icy calm, 'Move your foot. Get out of my life. And don't come back.'

He did not move his foot. 'I'll be leaving the city on Sunday and I won't be back. But in the meantime I'd very much like to spend some time with you.'

'You should buy yourself a self-help book on dating,' Joss said nastily. 'None of them will recommend leaving a woman alone at night on a city street in the pouring rain as a way of favourably impressing her. Or if it does, you should ask for your money back.'

He suddenly moved forward and took her by the shoulders, his face so close to hers that it was reduced to a harsh, unsparing geometry of planes and hollows. He said urgently, 'I had some bad news a couple of days ago and I've been in a foul mood ever since, Joss. I drank too much last night—which is not a habit of mine, believe me. I shouldn't have left you, I know I shouldn't. But I didn't know what else to do.' His smile was wry. 'The cabbie gave me hell, too.'

'You didn't even thank me for warning you about that car.' She remembered how it had appeared out of nowhere, its brakes screaming, its headlight like a single eye. 'It could have killed you,' she said, and in spite of herself her voice shook.

His jaw tightened. 'I suppose it could have,' he said with an intonation that puzzled her. 'If you saved my life, Joss, you could at least have a meal with me after work tonight.'

He was still standing near enough that she could have reached up and smoothed the lines from his forehead. She said stiltedly, 'That's illogical.'

His smile this time was disarming. 'You're no creature of logic, Joss—I know that from the way you sing.'

She realised with a flash of insight that what Niall had just said struck at the roots of her dilemma about her future. The research job represented the logical side of her character, the detached, scientific side that Great-Aunt Lucy would have despised; but when Joss thought of a medical career she thought of family medicine, which, practised well, took into account the whole person. 'I'm both,' she said stubbornly.

'You're a woman of deep emotion—I'd swear to it. If I'm waiting for you at nine o'clock, will you have a meal with me?'

In a thin voice Joss said, 'Are you married?'

Her question did not seem to surprise him. 'No. Nor
have I ever been.'

'How do I know that by nine o'clock you won't have
disappeared again?'

'I swear I won't.'

'Why, Niall?' she burst out. 'Why do you want to
spend time with me?'

Through the seams of her coat she felt his fingers
tighten. 'Because I can't help myself,' he said.

She believed him instantly and unequivocally. 'So you
feel it, too.'

'Oh, yes . . . you knew that, didn't you? I tried
running away, but that didn't work. So for two days I'd
like us to spend as much time together as we can.'

'Then you'll be leaving,' she said neutrally.

'And I won't be back. I want you to know that.' He
must have seen the doubt and frustration in her face,
because he added forcefully, 'Joss, I've never felt like
this with a woman before—never knew I could feel this
way. And believe me, that's no line. I almost wish it
were.' He gave a humourless laugh. 'For reasons of my
own, I couldn't have met you at a worse time.'

Joss hesitated, quite sure he would not share those
reasons. 'I've never felt this way, either,' she said.

'Maybe we'll find out we can't stand each other if we
spend more time together. That you love Italian food
and I love Chinese. That you're a morning person and
I'm a night person. That we're totally unsuited. It's
worth a try, isn't it?'

'You might sing off-key.'

'You might grind your teeth.'

'Or I might have false teeth,' Joss said primly.

Niall laughed outright. 'Just as long as your eyelashes
are real.'

She batted them demurely. 'A dollar forty-nine at the

cosmetics counter. Niall, that's only the second time
I've heard you laugh.'

His smile faded. 'We might find we have nothing in
common if we spend more time together. Or that we
even dislike each other.'

He had spoken without conviction. Joss said, 'And
what if we don't? What if we discover we both love
fettucini and hate egg rolls? And that I can make you
laugh? What then, Niall?' Her eyes searched his face.
'Will you still leave on Sunday?'

'I have to.'

In a spurt of anger she said, 'So where do you live,
Outer Mongolia? No postal service? No telephone?'

'When I leave on Sunday I won't be in touch with you
again,' Niall said inflexibly. 'So we can take the risk of
seeing each other for a couple of days, or else I'll leave
right now and I won't bother you again.'

'You're leaving the choice up to me? That's hardly
fair, when I have no idea why you have to leave!'

'All I can assure you is that you won't be hurting a
third person, Joss—there's no one else in my life.'

If she told him to leave he would do so, and she would
never know if the strange attraction between them was
real or unreal. But if she saw more of him and
discovered that the attraction was indeed real, what
then? Was he for some reason afraid of a close
relationship, and consequently playing his cards close to
his chest? Could she by Sunday make him change his
mind? She had no way of knowing.

With a feeling that she was stepping off a very high
cliff into thin air, Joss said quietly, 'I'll meet you here at
ten past nine.'

Briefly he rested his cheek on her hair. 'Thank you,'
he said equally quietly. 'Do you mind if I come into the
bar around eight?'

Not wanting to reveal how much his gesture had
affected her, she murmured, 'You must be getting bored

with my repertoire.'

'Not bored, Joss. Not with you.'

'Well . . .' she said inadequately. 'I'm going to be late again.'

'Off you go.' He reached round her for the door-handle.

The words were wrenched from her. 'Niall, I'm frightened.'

He made no attempt to touch her. 'If you want to back out, now's your chance.'

'Two days seem such a short time!'

'You can build up a lot of memories in two days,' he said harshly. 'Enough to last for a very long time. Or else you can play it safe and do nothing.'

'No. No, I don't want that.'

Niall's features gentled. 'It will be all right, Joss, you'll see.' He opened the door. 'I'll see you later.'

She slipped through the door, heard him close it behind her, and ran down the corridor. She had dreamed more than once of being balanced on the very edge of a perpendicular, pure white cliff. Sometimes she would glide through the air, lifted by invisible currents, bathed in sunlight. But other times she would fall, plummeting downwards with a scream tearing at her throat, knowing she would be dashed to pieces on the rocks below.

She was perched on the cliff-edge now; she could not have said which would be her fate.

CHAPTER THREE

PROMPTLY at eight o'clock Niall walked into the Red Lion. The pub was full, loud with conversation, thick with smoke. Joss had moved her stool by the piano, where she was surrounded by the usual Friday night group of singers, some of whom were in tune and some not. She saw Niall immediately, gave him a small, distracted smile and kept on playing. To her surprise he joined the group, adding his rich baritone to all the varied voices. He was very definitely in tune. They sang about the hole in Billy's bucket, the long way to Tipperary and the squid-jigging grounds; they waltzed around the billabong and deplored the houses made of ticky-tacky. Joss plucked her guitar and sang lustily and coached her group in the choruses; and in the small, still centre of her being was afraid. Nine o'clock, for once, came sooner than she would have wished. Without meeting Niall's eyes she said her goodbyes and fled to the staff room.

At exactly ten past nine she left the hotel by the side door, wearing a blue cotton jumpsuit and gold costume jewellery under her raincoat. Her eyes were very wide; her lips felt stiff. Niall was waiting for her, his collar turned up against the mist, his hair already damp. She had not been totally convinced he would be there. He said, 'You must be hungry, Joss.'

'Yes.'

'*Do* you like Italian food?'

She managed a smile. 'Yes.'

'Come on, then. I ate at this place on Monday; I think you'll like it.'

She scurried after him down the alley. The pavement was crowded. Niall took her arm, threaded it through his and kept on walking. His legs were much longer than hers. She trotted along at his side and said finally, 'Is the restaurant on fire?'

He slackened his pace. 'Sorry. I guess I'm in a hurry to have you sitting across from me at a table. No Mr Jodrey. No Tom. Just you and me. I made a reservation for nine-thirty.'

Joss could think of no reply to this. In a few minutes Niall led her down a flight of brick steps to a tiny restaurant in the cellar of an office building. Their table was tucked into a corner behind a white-washed pillar; Joss did not think this was coincidence. Scarlet geraniums bloomed in the deep window recesses, the tablecloths were red, and the seats very comfortable. Furthermore, no one was singing.

Niall said abruptly, 'Do you like to dance?'

'I love to.'

'Good, we'll go dancing after we eat. Tomorrow I thought we'd head out to the country.'

'I have to work.'

'Not until five.'

'I work at a bookshop in the day. From ten until four tomorrow.'

His eyes narrowed. 'Can't you get someone else to take your shift?'

'A couple of people owe me shifts. But——'

'Joss, we haven't got much time—let's not waste any of it. Phone someone now.'

Again she was afraid. Trying to disguise her feelings, she raised her eyebrows and said, 'Please, Joss?'

He laughed, took her hand and coaxed, 'Please, Joss.'

She'd climb a thirty-foot pole if he smiled at her like that. Or a tall white cliff. She went to the telephone, and on her second try got a replacement. When she went back to the table the waiter was there, and it took several minutes to choose what they would eat and drink. Then, finally, she and Niall were alone at the table. He raised his wineglass. 'To our time together, Joss.' Obediently she drank. He added softly, 'Relax. I'm not going to eat you.'

Joss put down her glass. But before she could say anything, Niall took her hands in his and spread them on the tablecloth. 'No rings,' he observed. 'Pretty fingernails—indisputably your own. What colour is the polish?'

'Almond Blush.'

'Nice. What's this scar?' He ran one finger along her left knuckle.

'I fell off the tractor when I was four. Jake got spanked for it, because he's the one who dared me to get up there.'

'Which brother is Jake?'

'The second youngest. My favourite, actually. Niall, what is this, an inquisition?'

He looked up. 'I have a lot to learn about you in a very short time.'

She had the sense of being on a roller-coaster that was travelling faster and faster. 'Communication's a two-way street,' she observed.

'As long as you don't ask why I have to leave on Sunday,' he said with suppressed violence. 'I know you don't understand. I can't make you understand. But we're together right now—and surely the present is what counts?'

With seeming irrelevance Joss said, 'You have the bluest eyes of anyone I've ever met,' and could see his instant relief that she was not pursuing the subject of Sunday.

He said with a boyish grin, 'And my lashes are my own—all part of the package.'

'You've got a scar on your thumb.'

He stretched out his right hand. Her brothers had all inherited their father's blunt fingers, but Niall's hand was long-fingered, beautiful to her in a way she had not thought a man's hand could be beautiful. His wrist was encircled by an elegant Swiss watch on a leather strap. He rubbed the sickle-shaped scar on his thumb and said, 'I got that playing hockey as a kid. Collided with the goal-post.'

Joss rested her chin on her hands, studying his features with secret pleasure. 'You have half a dozen grey hairs over each ear, a dent in your chin, and you're twenty-nine years old.'

He winced theatrically. 'Twenty-eight,' he said, adding with a wink, 'and eleven months. You're not a day over twenty-one.'

'I'm approximately one hundred and fifty days over twenty-one.'

'The youngest of a family of five.'

'Seven. I have two sisters as well.' She reeled off the names. 'Ross, Harvey, Glenis, Blanche, Jake, Gilbert, and me. Four of them married, three with children. I'm an aunt five times over. What about you?'

'You can't be an uncle if you have no brothers or sisters,' he said wryly.

It seemed a terrible fate to Joss to have grown up as an only child. 'Are your parents living?' she asked.

'My father is,' Niall said repressively. 'What are you doing in Toronto, Joss, when you're so homesick?'

She knew him well enough to realise that the subject of his parents was closed. Filing that fact for future reference, she explained about her research job and the funding cuts; this led to her decision about medical school versus a job in Halifax.

'If money were not a problem, which would you do?' Niall asked.

'Medical school,' she said promptly.

'Then do that. You'd make a very good doctor—that

disinterested kindness of yours. Besides, life's too short to find yourself caught in a job you don't want to do.'

'The voice of experience?' she ventured.

'I let myself get trapped in the fast lane. Executive in a big company, climbing to the top, working most nights and every weekend. Burn-out might be a fashionable term, but it's also a very real one.'

'The first time I met you I thought you looked exhausted.'

Niall did not elaborate, perhaps because their salads had arrived, tomatoes and basil in a garlic-flavoured dressing. Once the waiter had gone he said, 'Tell me more about your family.'

So Joss prattled on, bringing in her gypsy ancestress and Great-Aunt Lucy, the collie dog who never chased the cats and her mother's determined pursuit of her father forty years ago. As the man sitting across from her watched the play of emotion on her face, his blue eyes softened. Their salad plates were removed and replaced by bowls of linguini and Joss described some of the scrapes she had got into as a child. Niall remarked, 'Sounds like your brother Jake was the one who was always getting you into trouble—is that why he's your favourite?'

She twisted her wineglass. 'There was always an affinity between us, despite the eight-year age-difference. We even look alike. He's a widower now, with two little children. His wife died of cancer a year ago. He was so good to her . . . he took a leave of absence from his job so he could look after her at home, because she didn't want to go into hospital and be separated from the children. He was devastated when she died. But at least he had the satisfaction of knowing he'd done everything he could for her.'

'She demanded a lot of him,' Niall said harshly.

Joss looked up, surprised; somewhere she had touched a nerve. 'She did, yes. But he had a lot to give.

And they both knew that had he been the one who was
ill, she would have done the same for him.'

Niall shifted in his chair. 'It must have been hard on
the children,' he said, still with that harshness in his
voice.

'Of course it was. But at least they were involved in a
very real way. Death wasn't made into some unmentionable act that happens in hospitals.'

'I can't imagine that it was good for them having her
home,' he retorted.

'Then we'll have to disagree on that,' Joss rejoined
hotly. 'Because *I* think a very sad situation was handled
in the best possible way.' She took a gulp of Chianti.
'I'd much rather we disagreed over Chinese food than
over something as basic as death.'

'We knew this sort of thing might happen when we
agreed to spend the time together,' Niall answered
curtly.

Joss looked down at her plate. She considered herself
privileged to have witnessed the love between her
brother and his dying wife, and for Niall to view the
situation so differently upset her. She heard herself say,
'How did your mother die?'

'That's irrelevant.'

She sighed, pushing a clam around her plate,
suddenly finding the cellar room claustrophobic. 'Let's
go dancing,' she said. 'I don't want dessert.'

Niall made an obvious effort to speak more naturally.
'There's a Polish dance festival at the Harbourfront.
Dancing for the general public after ten o'clock. Want
to see what that's all about?'

'Sure,' Joss said agreeably, knowing they had
retreated from the cliff-edge on to safe ground again.
'Sounds like fun.'

The big hall was crowded with tables and chairs, a
colourful band on the stage playing the Polish equiva-
lent to a polka, the dance-floor crowded with gyrating

couples. Then costumed dancers circulated on the floor, helping to set up country dance sets. Joss and Niall joined three other couples. The steps were fairly simple, and in no time they were bobbing and hopping to the music, weaving in and out in increasingly intricate patterns. More couples joined in, so that for moments at a time Joss would lose sight of Niall. They danced a fast-moving polonaise that left her breathless, then the band struck up an old-fasioned waltz. She looked around the milling dancers for Niall's tall figure, not finding him, aware of a sudden anxiety. He couldn't have disappeared. He wouldn't do that. Edging off the dance-floor, she searched for him among the tables.

He was sitting on a chair against the wall, hunched over. She pushed between the tables, almost ran the last few feet, and knelt beside him. 'Niall! What's wrong?'

His face was deathly pale, his features contorted. 'Stitch,' he gasped. 'Happens sometimes.'

There was sweat on his forehead. She pulled a tissue from her pocket and wiped his brows; his hands were pressed to his ribs. 'Should I get a doctor?'

'No. I'll be fine.' Her face was very close to his; he muttered, 'Don't look so worried, Joss. I've let myself get out of shape the last year or so, that's all.'

He straightened slowly. His breathing seemed easier, and she let out her own breath in a sigh of relief. 'You frightened me.'

'Sorry. My own fault—should have been jogging every noon hour instead of chaining myself to a desk.'

'You're too thin. I bet you don't eat properly.'

'Yes, Mother,' he said with the ghost of a smile.

Joss blushed and spoke the literal truth. 'I don't want to be your mother!'

'Any Freudian worth his salt would be glad to hear

you say that.'

She giggled. 'I think you've recovered.'

'So much so that we should dance this waltz together.' Niall stood up. 'It seems suitably lethargic.'

She loved it when he assumed that deadpan expression. As they reached the edge of the dance-floor, Niall took her in his arms. He had left his sweater and trench coat at the coat check; his shirt-sleeves were rolled up. Joss rested one hand on his shoulder, felt him take her hand, and began to dance.

Within ten seconds she knew she was in trouble. Beneath her palm she could feel the shift of his shoulder muscles; he was holding her closely because the floor was crowded, and the contact made her tingle from head to toe. Although she had pictured an embrace in the orchard, it had somehow never involved the actuality of a man's body: bone and muscles, movement, flexibility and strength. Someone bumped into her from behind, thrusting her against Niall's chest; his arm tightened around her waist. She closed her eyes and knew she had never understood the meaning of desire before.

The waltz ended with flourish on the accordion. Into her ear Niall muttered, 'You're dynamite, Jocelyn Gayle. I think we'd better go for a good brisk walk.'

'Or a swim in Lake Ontario.'

'So it was mutual? I wasn't the only one consumed by lust?' Joss had been staring at his shirt-front. He lifted her chin, saw the shyness and confusion in her hazel eyes and added, 'You don't need to answer—I can read your mind.'

'I hope not!'

He chuckled. 'Apart from the fact that you make me feel like Tristan, Antony and Romeo all rolled up in one, do you know what's the nicest thing about you? You make me laugh.'

She was still standing in the circle of his arms. 'I don't think you've done much laughing recently.'

'No, I haven't.'

'You haven't told me what the bad news was,' she said, and felt the tensing of his muscles.

'Another closed area, Joss.'

'There are a lot of them,' she said, carefully keeping her voice light.

'Yes.'

'I've talked more about myself than you have about you.'

'I hope you'll continue to do so. You're like a breath of fresh air for me.'

Her brain was buzzing with questions, none of which she asked. 'So what's it to be next—the walk or the swim?'

'The lake's polluted, they say. So we could settle on a walk, couldn't we? Unless you're tired?'

'No, I'm fine.'

In a very real way Joss was telling the truth. Despite all the closed areas, she felt that she and Niall had made enormous strides that evening, for Niall, the most secretive of men, had acknowledged that she was good for him and that he desired her. Sunday began to seem like less of a barrier. Of her own volition she tucked her arm in his when they went outside; he smiled down at her, resting his own hand over hers.

Along the waterfront crowds of people surged and eddied like flotsam caught in invisible currents. Joss, used to a rural environment, found the constant movement, the raucous voices and loud music, the unavoidable body contact, fascinating for a while but ultimately wearying. After half an hour or so she said to Niall, 'If you like we could go to my apartment for coffee. My roommate's out right now, but she'll be home a little later.'

Niall stopped, looking down at her. The mist had turned her hair into a tangle of curls. 'Despite what happened on the dance-floor, I'm not going to jump on you, Joss.'

She knew she had been transparent: country girl in the big city. 'And what if I jump on you?' she said with attempted airiness.

'I might call for help. But then again, I might not.' He reached down and smoothed her cheek. 'You're blushing.'

'Your hands are cold.' She held his fingers to the warmth of her skin, and the crowds dropped away as if they did not exist. Niall said roughly, 'Let's go to your apartment. I won't jump on you, I swear.' His smile was crooked. 'I've always been known to have a strong will. But I would like to be alone with you.'

She wanted the same. Fifteen minutes later, after a journey during which neither of them said very much, she was ushering Niall in the door of her apartment. Nasturtium, curled up on the chair, opened her eyes, yawned, and went back to sleep.

'Some chaperon,' said Niall.

Joss knew, which Niall did not, that Nasturtium would be their only chaperon for at least two hours; Magda was always late on Friday nights. The apartment seemed very quiet. It was, she realised, the first time she and Niall had ever been truly alone. She took his coat and hung it in the closet. 'Sorry about the mess, my roommate isn't what you'd call tidy. All the furniture is hers, I'm just living here for the summer, she's getting married in the fall. She's the one who got me the job at the Red Lion, she's a singer, too——'

Niall put a hand on her shoulder as if he was soothing a frightened animal. 'Slow down,' he said.

'I'm acting as though you're my first date!' Joss wailed. 'You look so calm and collected.'

'Then I'm a good actor. Do you think I'm not aware that we're alone in this apartment and that behind those two doors there are undoubtedly beds and that I'd like to be in one of them with you? Of course I would. But we're not going to do that, Joss; it wouldn't be right. So why don't you put the kettle on and tell me what the cat's name is. I've always liked cats—such self-contained creatures.'

'Like you,' Joss said with a tiny smile. 'Regular coffee or decaffeinated?'

She busied herself in the kitchen, trying not to think about the beds, and put some of Magda's delicious almond cookies on a tray with the coffee. She and Niall sat decorously on the chesterfield and talked sensibly about the state of the world, while Naturtium purred away on Niall's lap. When they had finished Niall carried the tray back into the kitchen for her, Nasturtium following close behind; Nasturtium had taken a fancy to Niall.

The kitchen was very small, made more so by Magda's collection of cookbooks. Niall pulled out a book on Moroccan cooking, saying absently, 'I spent a summer in Rabat with the company several years ago.'

Joss rinsed out the mugs, reached behind her for the cookie tin and stepped on Nasturtium's tail. Nasturtium yowled. Joss leaped clear of the cat, stumbled against Niall and suddenly found herself locked in his arms. The cookie tin fell off the counter and clanged on the floor. Niall said roughly, 'Very appropriate sound effects.' Then he kissed her.

At some level Joss had known since the beginning of the evening that this would happen, and she welcomed it with all her heart. Trustingly she closed her eyes, put her arms around his neck and kissed him back.

The cookie tin rolled into a corner, fell on its side and was still. Nasturtium muttered away to herself in a disgruntled fashion. But for Joss there was nothing but the strength of Niall's embrace, the warmth of his lips, and the clean, masculine scent of his skin. Paradoxically she felt as though she had everything in the world to

learn, yet knew all there was to know. She moulded her
body to his and parted her lips to the dart of his tongue.
Nasturtium, looking affronted, jumped up on the counter
and butted her head hard into Niall's ribs.

Taken by surprise, Niall raised his head just as
Nasturtium dug her claws into his sweater and stretched
lazily. He glowered at the cat. 'Did I say you weren't much
good as a chaperon?' he growled. 'I take it all back.'

Joss gave a shaky laugh. 'I think we must have ruined
the rest of the almond cookies, as well.'

'To say nothing of my equanimity.'

Niall's eyes were pools of blue, fiercely alive. 'Who
jumped on who?' Joss asked.

He ran his fingers around his collar; she could see the
pulse pounding at the base of his throat and wondered if
hers was doing the same. 'We could debate it,' he said. 'Or
we could blame it on the cat. What time did you say your
roommate gets home?'

Joss wanted him to kiss her again. She would swear
Niall had been shaken by his passionate response to her,
and she did not know how else to attack his reticence or
weaken his defences. Sex was not a weapon she would
have chosen had there been unlimited time. But always, at
the back of her mind, hovered the thought of Sunday. She
said truthfully, 'Magda doesn't get home until two on
Fridays and Saturdays. She sings in a club, you see, so her
hours are different from mine.'

Niall was frowning. 'Did you say her name was Magda?
What's her last name?'

'Trevanian. She sings in the Coq d'Or.'

'Will you be seeing her tonight?' he rapped. 'Or
tomorrow?'

Puzzled, Joss said, 'I probably won't see her now until
Monday . . . we almost never connect at week-
ends because she spends the days with her fiancé.
Why?'

Niall gave his head a little shake. 'The name seems

familiar, that's all. Joss, I should be going.'

The man so officiously looking at his watch did not seem like the man who had kissed her so hungrily a few moments ago. Unable to disguise a crushing disappointment, Joss faltered, 'Already?'

'It's late.'

'Is there something wrong?'

He must have seen the distress in her face. 'There's nothing wrong. But I mustn't kiss you like that again or we'll end up making love on the floor among the almond cookies.'

Even though she knew he had not really answered her question, she valiantly tried to match his tone. 'With Nasturtium watching every move.'

'You know what they say—three's a crowd.'

Joss trailed after him into the living-room and watched him take his coat off the hanger. She felt tired and confused, not nearly as sure of her ability to alter the events of Sunday as she had been a few moments ago. 'So I haven't done anything to offend you?' she burst out.

He turned to face her. 'On the contrary,' he said slowly. 'Everything about you delights me. Which is, of course, part of the problem. What time will I pick you up tomorrow, Joss?'

'Any time after nine.'

'One minute past.'

'So you do want to spend the day with me?'

'Are you seriously doubting that?'

'I don't know what I think any more,' she said with unhappy truth.

'We'll have a good day, Joss—a day to remember.' He leaned forward and kissed her briefly on the lips. 'Sleep well.'

The door latched behind him. Joss turned the key in the lock then leaned her back against the door. The room looked very empty without him. Of what use were memories, she thought painfully, when what she wanted was the real man?

CHAPTER FOUR

Joss woke early the next morning with all her optimism renewed. She still had Saturday and Sunday, two more days of Niall's company; remembering that explosive kiss by the kitchen counter, she could not believe he would simply get on a plane and disappear. She sang in the shower, dressed in her prettiest flowered skirt and her newest sandals, and purposely chose a low-necked knitted top to go with the skirt. She put her swimsuit, sweater and running sneakers into a canvas bag, and was down on the pavement waiting when Niall pulled up at two minutes to nine.

He reached across and opened the passenger door. 'You're early,' he said. She smiled at him, a smile as bright as the morning sunshine, and leaned over to throw her bag on the back seat. He added in a stifled voice, 'What are you trying to do to me, Joss?'

She glanced at him in surprise, realised that she had presented him with an unobstructed view of her cleavage, and turned scarlet. She sat down hurriedly. 'I've got a shirt that buttons to the collar with long sleeves,' she babbled. 'I could go and change.'

'Please don't,' he said. 'I like the view.'

That she had chosen the low neckline on purpose made matters worse. Joss did up her seat-belt and said, 'This is a nice car. Is it yours?'

'Rented. Aren't you going to kiss me good morning?'

She had recovered a little of her poise. 'Do you think we should? Nasturtium isn't here.'

'Let's risk it.'

His lips were warm and made demands Joss was only

58

too ready to respond to. She murmured against his mouth, 'At lunch time you could kiss me good afternoon. If you want to.'

'Seems a long time to wait. How about every hour on the hour?'

'Better and better.' The sunlight seemed to be coming from within her, enveloping her in its brilliance. Joss said impulsively, 'At this precise moment I am completely and absolutely happy.'

'Oh, God, Joss,' Niall said helplessly.

She had never seen such a combination of naked longing and frustration in a man's face before. 'Shouldn't I have said that?'

'You took me aback, that's all. I'm happy to be with you, too.'

But behind his smile, fleetingly, was a shadow that no smile could have erased, the shadow of an unhappiness deeper than words. Joss saw it and then it was gone, and she was left to wonder if she had imagined it. Feeling as though in a few short seconds she had run the gamut from joy to pain, she said prosaically, 'Where are we going?' and then wondered if he would see her question as a *double entendre*.

Apparently he did not. 'To the country.'

'I haven't been outside the city since I came here. Show me a cow and I'll probably embrace it.'

'Just as long as it isn't a bull.'

'I do know the difference,' Joss said, glancing at him through her lashes. 'I've known it ever since my brother Jake watched a movie about rodeos and tried to go for a ride on my dad's Holstein bull . . . I was about five at the time. The bull, needless to say, was not happy. Neither was Jake when my dad had finished with him.'

As they drove north on Yonge Street she chattered on about the farm. But when they pulled up at a traffic light by a fashionable dress shop, she exclaimed, 'Drive on quickly—that's exactly the raincoat I'd like to own. The only thing wrong with it is the price.'

Obligingly the light changed to green. 'That shiny blue one?' Niall asked.

'Mmm . . . two hundred and twenty dollars. I priced them downtown.'

'You'd look nice in it.'

'I know I would.' Joss sighed. 'You know, that's another reason against medical school. I'm awfully tired of scrimping and saving. I'd like to buy that raincoat with a jazzy umbrella to go with it and knee-high boots. I'd like to own six pairs of Italian shoes, all different colours, and at least two pairs of leather boots . . . if I go to med school I'll be lucky if I can afford a pair of socks.'

'But those are kind of transitory things, aren't they?'

'The first time I met you you were wearing a very expensive suit.'

'That's true—so I suppose it's easy for me to say clothes aren't important.' Niall glanced over at her. 'They're not, though, Joss. It's where they carry you that's far more important.'

'OK. But I'd also like to help my brother Gilbert with his new business and buy my mum and dad a VCR.'

'Perhaps by going to medical school you'll be giving them something they really want . . . money isn't always the most meaningful gift. Your parents sound like the kind of people who'd be proud to have a doctor in the family. And I know you're not interested in it for the money.'

Joss looked at him thoughtfully; everything he had said made sense. 'So did you work as hard as you did for the money?'

'Power, more likely. Ambition. Although money went along with it, of course. It's a rat race, Joss, believe me.'

'What will you do next?'

His hands tightened on the wheel. 'I don't know. I

haven't given it a lot of thought.'

'You have to get out of the city in order to think,' she said darkly.

He laughed. 'So you'll be brainstorming among the bulls, will you?'

'I haven't got long to make up my mind. A week at the most.'

Niall gave her a heart-warming smile. 'You'll do the right thing, Joss, I know you will. You're a good person.'

'You will, too,' she said slowly. 'It will be more difficult for you, somehow—although I don't know why I'm saying that.'

'My choices are much narrower,' he said with sudden savage emphasis. 'That's why. Let's not talk about it, Joss. I want to enjoy the day with you.'

The words were out before she had time to think. 'Are you in trouble with the law?'

'God, no!'

'That's one way of having your choices narrowed.'

'Joss, dear, I am neither a Hell's Angel nor a Mafioso—scout's honour. Tell me more about your brother Gilbert and your two sisters.'

As they drove north across the flat countryside she complied. An hour later they left the main road for a side road. The industrial sites had been left behind; the land was hilly, with groves of trees clustered in the valleys; the first farmhouse appeared. Niall said, 'There's a cow. Want to give it a hug?'

'It's a she and that's an electric fence . . . I think I can restrain myself. Oh, Niall, this is wonderful! It's the *country*—you don't know how much I've missed it.'

'We'll stop in a while and go for a walk.'

They meandered on, taking side roads at random until they came to a narrow dirt road that followed a river. Niall parked the car in the shade of an oak tree. 'Want to walk? We could take our swimsuits.'

The road was roofed by the spreading limbs of old elms, while the river whispered to itself, its brown waters overhung by willows. A kingfisher preened on a sunlit branch. The air smelled of river water and ferns and the damp carpet of leaves from many autumns. When Niall took Joss's hand she knew again the clarity of perfect happiness.

Round the first corner they came to the driveway of an old farm set well back from the road. Two little girls were riding their bicycles up and down the driveway; a third, younger, was wrestling red-faced with a yellow skipping rope that had entangled itself in the spokes of her tricycle. She was plainly on the verge of bursting into tears.

Niall said calmly, 'I can get that out for you if you like.'

She eyed him distrustfully, like a puppy about to bolt. 'It's stuck,' she said, and jammed her thumb in her mouth.

Niall knelt down beside the tricycle, which was battered enough to have belonged to each of the older girls. 'You did a job on it, didn't you?' he said, his long fingers setting to work on a knot. 'My name's Niall. What's yours?' With a grunt of satisfaction he loosened the first knot.

The child removed her thumb, said, 'Kimberley Dawn *Rut*ledge,' and replaced it. She had a mop of brown curls and pugnacious little features. Joss had the feeling that Kimberley Dawn had to fight for what she wanted; certainly her two sisters were paying no attention to her predicament.

Patiently Niall worked away, chatting to the child as he did so. She crept closer, until the two brown heads were very close together, both bent over the front wheel of the tricycle. Joss watched with a lump in her throat, for this was a side to Niall she had not seen before. He spoke to the child without condescension, yet with quiet kindness; for a crazy moment she found herself fantasising that Kimberley Dawn was their own child, hers and Niall's. She would like to have Niall's child, she thought blankly. That, too, felt right.

Niall pulled the last few inches of the skipping rope free of the wheel. 'There you go,' he said.

'Lotsa knots in it,' said Kimberley Dawn.

'Want me to take them out?'

'Yup.'

It took him about five minutes. But finally he handed the rope back to the child. 'That's better.'

She smiled for the first time, a smile that brought radiance to her grubby face. Opening her palm, she disclosed a small, black rock. 'I found this,' she said solemnly. 'You can have it.'

'Thank you,' Niall said with equal solemnity, and took the rock. 'Goodbye, Kimberley Dawn.'

'Bye.' She threw the rope on the ground, jumped on the tricycle and pedalled furiously up the driveway after her two sisters. For a moment Niall stood watching her, something so forbidding in the set of his profile that Joss looked away; his thoughts, whatever they were, were intensely private. She picked up the skipping rope, wound it in a neat coil, and put it back on the ground. 'You did a good job,' she said easily.

'Cute kid.' He suddenly hunched his shoulders. 'Let's find somewhere to swim.'

Within ten minutes they came to a bend in the river where a bank of shale edged a deep pool. A robin was singing in the thicket; the sun bronzed the water. 'Perfect,' said Joss. 'I can get changed in those bushes.'

'You go first.'

She scrambled into the ditch, scratching her bare legs on the alders. Once she was hidden from view she took off her clothes, adding more scratches to her anatomy. Her swimsuit was an abbreviated one-piece, brilliantly flowered. As she looked down at herself she wished there were a few more flowers, for what had seemed sophisticated in the store now seemed merely brazen. She draped the towel strategically, put her clothes in her bag and inched her way out of the bushes on to the shale. Niall was watching her from the roadside. After she waved at him he disappeared into the alders.

Joss spread her towel on the smoothest part of the bank and sat down. Her surroundings, with their myriad shades of green and ever-shifting patterns of sun and shadow, were very peaceful, yet she felt absurdly self-conscious. She had always taken her body for granted, considering privately that her legs were too long and her breasts rather too full, certainly when compared to the willowy models who were so fashionable; but she had never worried about it overmuch. Now she was wondering what Niall would think of her, discovering that his opinion mattered quite inordinately.

Branches rustled behind her, and she heard footsteps on the shale. She looked round. Niall's body was tanned and rangy, his chest a tangle of dark hair, his legs long and muscular. Very muscular for someone who claimed to be out of shape, she thought doubtfully. Then she saw the narrow red scar that curved around his ribs and forgot her suspicions. She said sharply, 'What happened there?'

He bent to spread out his towel and said, his back to her, 'I was involved in an accident. They had to operate.'

So was the accident a clue to all his silences? she wondered, and knew she lacked the courage to ask. Turning, Niall reached out a hand to her. Slowly she stood up. Their hands still linked, he let his eyes wander over her, and there was in them such a mingling of pleasure and desire that unconsciously Joss stood taller. He said huskily, 'I can't get over how beautiful you are. And yet I knew you would be.' He kissed the tip of her nose. 'Time for a swim—the water had better be cold.'

The water was wonderfully refreshing. They swam quietly, because the serenity of the woodland pool somehow precluded noisy horseplay, and then walked back up on the bank. Joss lay back on her towel. 'Wonderful,' she said lazily. 'Who needs shiny raincoats?'

'You look much nicer as you are.'

Niall had spread his towel next to hers and was leaning on one elbow, watching her. She said, 'Your eyes are the colour of the sky.'

'Yours are the same colour as the river. Mud-brown,' he teased. But then he added, 'Joss . . . beautiful Joss,' and leaned over to kiss her.

It was a kiss suffused with sunlight and the songs of birds, as gentle and deep as the river; it lasted for a long time. His chest was touching her wet swimsuit. She stroked the smooth, wet planes of his back and knew that in a place many miles from the orchard she had come home.

He covered her with his body and kissed her again, more intensely, almost with desperation. With one hand he cupped her breast; her legs were tangled with his so that she felt against her thigh the hardness that was the essence of his desire. She kissed him back, trying to tell him with her lips and the surrendering curve of her body that he was the only man in the world for her. But then, so suddenly that she was shocked, Niall lifted himself off, his face only inches from hers, his rapid breathing stirring her hair. 'We've got to stop,' he said hoarsely. 'I don't want to, but we must.'

She felt bereft. But more important than her own feelings was the torment in his eyes, a mixture of pain and terrible longing that caught at her throat. Wanting to make him smile, she moved her thigh very slightly and said, 'I know you don't want to stop.'

Some of the tension relaxed in his face. 'No secrets,

huh? Joss, I want to make love to you, I don't have to tell you that. But I'm leaving tomorrow and I can't have a one-day fling with you. Whatever it is that's between us isn't casual—at least not for me.'

She answered his unspoken question. 'Nor is it for me.'

She was not altogether unhappy that he had pulled away. Never having met the right man before, she had never made love before, either, and when she and Niall did make love she wanted them both to feel right about it. She was increasingly sure that they would make love, for mingled with the hunger in his eyes there had been tenderness. Their relationship, which had begun with so much conflict, had become far more intimate today; and she cherished Niall's honesty with her. By tomorrow, she thought confidently, she would understand the source of his reticence.

She said, smiling, 'I'm hungry. For food.'

'As well as . . .?'

'As well as. Sublimation, you call it.'

'I could do with a good dollop of sublimation right now.' Niall traced her cheekbone with one finger. 'So you figure a hamburger will be an adequate distraction?'

'Along with a chocolate fudge sundae with whipped cream and nuts.'

'You left out the french fries.'

Joss loved to see him laugh, for it always made him look years younger. 'And the ketchup,' she said.

His fingertip had moved to the curve of her eyelid. He peered suspiciously at her eyes. 'Those lashes weren't a dollar forty-nine at the drugstore. They're the real McCoy.'

She chuckled. 'They always were. I put mascara on to make them longer.'

'The better to trip me with.'

She said soulfully, 'A million-dollar industry just so

I'll catch myself a man.'

'You'd have tripped me up without the mascara, Joss.' His smile faded. He hugged her to his chest with all his strength, his face buried in her damp hair, and muttered, 'I wish to God I'd met you five years ago.'

She would have been sixteen five years ago. But she did not remind him of this. Instead she held him as hard as she could, feeling anxiety drive away her confidence, knotting itself within her as tightly as the tangles in Kimberley Dawn's skipping rope. Something was wrong, horribly wrong; she had known that from the beginning. She had to find out what it was. 'Niall,' she said, her voice smothered against his chest, 'can't you tell me what's the trouble? No matter what it is, I'll do my best to understand.'

'I can't, Joss—it's too late. And it wouldn't be fair.'

'What you're doing now hardly seems fair.'

He raised his head. 'I warned you yesterday that this is the way it would be.'

'I didn't realise it would be so difficult.'

He levered himself off her and tweaked her hair; but his smile did not reach his eyes. 'It's as difficult as we make it,' he said dismissively, getting to his feet and pulling her up to face him. 'Let's go find that chocolate fudge sundae.'

She met his gaze. 'I'll never forget this place,' she said with total sincerity.

He flinched. *'Don't*, Joss.'

'Will you?' she persisted ruthlessly.

For a brief moment all his anger showed. 'You don't have to ask that question—you know the answer already.'

'I wanted to hear you say it.'

'No, I won't forget this place! No, I won't forget you. Are you satisfied?'

'This is a crazy game we're playing,' Joss said in a small voice. 'I keep breaking the rules because I don't

understand the necessity for them. I don't even
understand why you won't make love to me.'

'I explained that to you.'

'I think you're afraid to!'

'I told you the truth, I swear.' His smile was wintry.
'You know as well as I do the times we live in . . . I am not
carrying any unmentionable communicable diseases, and
I've all the appetites of a normal man. Tomorrow I may
well kick myself for being so goddamned noble . . . but
that's the way I want to play it.'

His will was like a steel door, totally impenetrable.
Again Joss wondered if she would be able to find the
key in the short time she had, and felt a flicker of terror.
She fought it down, for she was not one to admit defeat
easily. 'I'll get changed,' she said. 'Then we'll go in
search of that sundae.'

'Thanks, Joss,' Niall said, making no attempt to
camouflage his relief.

They walked back along the river road almost in
silence; the three little girls were nowhere to be seen. But
when they were driving to the nearest town in search of
a restaurant they passed a dairy farm where a mixed
herd of Holsteins and Guernseys were grazing in a field
that bordered on the road. Without being asked, Niall
pulled over. Joss got out and walked over to the fence, a
newly painted white-board fence that her father could
not have afforded. Three or four cows ambled over to
investigate, blowing at her shirt-front through grass-
stained nostrils and suffering her to scratch their bony
foreheads. 'This is a really good herd,' she said to Niall,
and began explaining some of the technicalities of milk
production. The shadow that had lain across her spirits
since the embrace on the riverbank vanished,
particularly when Niall asked some purposely dim-
witted questions, and they were in perfect accord when
they got back in the car. They ate in a country inn beside
the river and afterwards wandered hand in hand

through some ornamental gardens on the outskirts of the town. As they walked under an archway overhung with frothy, cream-coloured roses, Joss inhaled with delight. 'They must be an old-fashioned variety; the newer ones never seem to smell, do they?'

Niall cupped a blossom in his hand. 'I've always had a yen to grown roses,' he said absently.

'Why don't you, then? It would be one way to quit the rat race.'

'A surefire way, I should think.' He suddenly grasped her shoulder so tightly that she almost cried out with pain, and muttered, 'When I'm with you, I forget . . .'

Joss stood very still; the sunlight gleamed in his thick dark hair. 'Forget what, Niall?'

He dropped his forehead to her shoulder. In a muffled voice he said, 'Hold on, Joss . . . just hold on.'

She put her arms around him, feeling the tension in his shoulders, hearing his rapid, shallow breathing. A rose brushed her elbow; an ant was crawling up the pink-tinged, velvety petal. She watched it absorbedly until she had conquered the urge to cry out, 'What's wrong, Niall? Tell me what's wrong!' Instead she said softly, rocking him in her arms, 'It's all right, I'm here . . . I won't let go,' and prayed that no one would disturb them.

No one did. Her arms were cramped by the time Niall raised his head. He said almost inaudibly, 'You comfort me, Joss.'

'Niall, please——'

He shook his head. 'Don't ask. For God's sake, don't ask.'

She could not possibly have persisted, for something tight-held in his face forbade it. She said gently, 'Maybe you need to grow some roses, Niall—it would give you the time to sort out whatever's wrong.'

He straightened to his full height, rubbing at the back of his neck, his eyes avoiding hers. 'Time is exactly what

I need,' he said in an emotionless voice. 'Talking of time, shouldn't we head back to the city? You have to be at work at five.'

She did not want to go back to work, thought Joss, as they strolled across the grass towards the car, Niall's arm looped around her shoulders. What she wanted to do was book a room in the nearest inn, take Niall to bed with her and hold him in her arms. Maybe they would make love. But her motives would not be a simple matter of desire . . .

She said nothing of this, and sat quietly on the drive home, her hand resting on his knee; the physical contact was a link between them all the more powerful for being unacknowledged. Niall dropped her off at the apartment, promising to meet her at the Red Lion midway through her performance. She showered, changed and took the subway to the hotel.

The bar was packed, the noise level the usual dull roar for a Saturday night, the smokers much in evidence. Feeling horribly out of place, Joss began to sing. She did not want to be in the Red Lion singing songs she had sung a hundred times before. She wanted to be with Niall. Even when he arrived about quarter past seven her mood did not much improve. His face was only one among many; and, according to him, it would be his last visit to the pub.

Nine o'clock came. She ran to the staff room, changed into her most stylish dress, a tangerine linen belted at the waist and worn with a pristine white jacket, and hurried to the side door. Niall was waiting for her; impetuously she threw her arms around him, burrowing into his chest and creasing the linen.

'I was afraid you might not be here . . . oh, Niall, I've got lipstick on your shirt.'

'I said I'd be here.'

'I know you did. But I keep thinking I'm going to wake up and find out this has all been a dream.' She fished in her bag for a tissue and scrubbed at his shirt, frowning in concentration, her tongue between her teeth. 'There,' she said finally, 'that's better.'

Glancing up, she caught him looking at her with such concentrated emotion that she totally forgot whatever she had been about to say. He said flatly, 'Despite everything, I'll never be sorry we met, Joss. Never. You've taught me such a lot.'

'I *have*?'

'You're so real. You're rooted in sanity, in the kind of values I'd almost forgotten—if indeed I ever knew them.' Briefly he squeezed her hand. 'Thank you.'

His words had a finality that frightened Joss. Burying her fear, for there was still tomorrow, she mumbled, 'I was only myself.'

'Never say only.' He tucked her arm in his. 'I made a reservation at Scarlatti's.'

Scarlatti's was one of the most chic places to eat in Toronto; being on a budget, Joss had never been there. Glad that she had worn her tangerine dress, she said fliply, 'I should have put on more mascara.'

'Or your dollar-forty-nine lashes.'

Niall was wearing a tailored summerweight suit that enhanced his dark good looks; his arm felt substantial under her palm, a reality of flesh and blood that could not possibly disappear. 'Let's go!' she said brightly.

The ceiling of Scarlatti's main dining-room was made of glass, while a fountain surrounded by orchids splashed into a pool in the middle of the tiled floor. Potted plants in a profusion of colours climbed a spiral staircase against one wall, their petals glowing in the candlelight; fig trees garlanded with tiny lights branched to the rooftop. 'You've brought me to the country again, Niall,' Joss exclaimed, clasping her hands in childlike wonder.

'I thought you'd like it here.'

Again they had a corner table, alongside some magnificent bird of paradise plants, the flowers like exotic orange and purple butterflies. Joss sat quietly, letting all the colours sink into her consciousness. 'My sister Blanche would like this restaurant,' she said eventually. 'She's the gardener of the family; she lives in Vancouver. It seems a little crude to think of actually eating here.'

'Don't let the waiter hear you say that—he'd be insulted.'

Joss managed to eat quite a lot, however, because the preparation of the food matched the care that had been taken with the décor. Throughout the meal she and Niall avoided personal subjects by unspoken consent, discussing everything from movies to music, and politics to plays. Again Joss was happy, and it showed in the light in her eyes and the lilt in her laughter; Niall watched her, playing with his wineglass, his own face unusually contented.

It was midnight when they left Scarlatti's. The street seemed very bare after the lush interior of the restaurant; they strolled along arm in arm in no particular direction until they came to University Avenue, Joss's favourite street in the city. Along the boulevard little white lights twinkled on the trees, with the imposing buildings of the university on either side. 'You can hardly see the stars in the city,' said Joss. 'Maybe that's why so many places use those lights. We should go the museum tomorrow, Niall, it's not far from here—I love the dinosaur exhibit.'

'I'm leaving tomorrow, Joss—I told you that.'

'Not first thing in the morning,' she teased. 'You said we had two days, so I've got all kinds of plans for tomorrow.'

Niall had stopped on the pavement. He said evenly, 'I meant yesterday and today, Joss. My plane leaves early tomorrow morning.'

She gazed at him in consternation. 'You mean tonight is it? I won't see you tomorrow at all?'

Trying to joke, he said, 'It's already tomorrow. But you won't see me in the morning, no.'

She unlinked her sleeve from his and crossed her arms over her breast; she felt very cold. 'You're going to give me your address and your phone number, though, aren't you?'

'No, Joss. Don't you remember what I said? No further contact after this weekend.'

'But that was before we spent so much time together! Didn't you enjoy yourself today?'

'Of course I did. But——'

'Deny that you're attracted to me.'

'I can't deny that and be honest with you. Anyway, there'd be no sense in denying it—I made it fairly obvious down by the river, didn't I?'

Her heart was beating in sick, heavy thuds, as if she was fighting for her very life. 'It's more than sexual attraction, Niall—I'd swear it is. We're right together, you and I, in all ways. Not just sex.'

He said tightly, 'We didn't make love today—so how can we know that we're even right together as far as sex is concerned?'

'You're playing with words!' Another couple was approaching them on the pavement. Joss waited until they were past, then resumed in a furious whisper, 'I've never made love, but I would have today with you——'

'You've *never* made love?' Niall interrupted.

'I'm a throwback to the Victorian age—twenty-one-year-old virgin. And do you know why? Because I'd never met the right man. Until last Wednesday, that is.'

A spasm crossed his face. 'Don't, Joss—please don't!'

'It's true, every word.' She suddenly clasped his sleeve. 'Niall, you can tell me I'm crazy if you like—but I'm convinced you and I could fall in love very easily. And I don't mean just for a week or a month or even a year. I mean for a lifetime.'

His laugh grated on her nerves. 'People don't fall in love for a lifetime any more, Joss. Look at the statistics on the divorce rate.'

'Yes, they do. People like me. And people like you.'

Her eyes searched his face for the slightest sign of relenting and found none. She dropped his arm and said in a voice she scarcely recognised as her own, 'I'm not asking much, Niall. Only that you keep in touch in some small way. But please don't just vanish from my life.' In spite of herself her voice broke. 'I don't think I could bear that.'

Niall had shoved his hands in his pockets. Deep lines scored his cheeks. Cutting off each word, he said, 'That was the agreement.'

'Don't talk to me about agreements!' Joss cried wildly. 'Was it in the agreement that you kiss me the way you did beside the river? Or laugh with me all day? Or look at me with love—yes, love, dammit!—when you met me at the hotel this evening? Agreements are for lawyers and business executives, Niall—not for living, breathing people like you and me that have blood in their veins and care about each other!'

'This had gone far enough, Joss,' he snarled. 'Come on, I'm going to take you home.'

She struck away his hand. 'You haven't answered my questions.'

'Nor do I intend to.'

She spread her hands in utter helplessness. 'What do I have to do to get through to you?'

'You can't.'

The two words fell like stones into the depths of her heart. 'You mean that, don't you?' Joss whispered.

'Yes.'

'You've never even told me your name.' She pressed her palms to her cheeks, terrified that she was going to weep. 'Can't you at least tell me why?'

He held her impaled in the bitter blue of his eyes and

said loudly, 'I lied when I told you I wasn't married. I am married, Joss—and I'll never leave my wife.'

For a split second Joss thought he was telling the truth. Then she said evenly, 'I don't believe you. I'd know if you had a wife.'

'Feminine intuition?' he sneered.

'I'd know.' She made one last attempt. 'Niall, please just give me your name and where you're from. I won't bother you or chase you, I promise—but at least I'll know.'

'No, Joss.'

'Just your name!' she begged.

'No!'

The cruellest word in the language. 'I can't believe you're doing this to me.'

'You knew all along that I would—you just chose to avoid the truth.'

Joss took a deep, shuddering breath. 'Then it's over, isn't it?' she said in a dead voice. 'Over before it's begun.' Briefly she closed her eyes, willing herself not to cry. When she opened them they were brilliant with unshed tears. 'I suppose all that's left is to thank you for the two happiest days of my life. And to wish you well, Niall.'

She could not force herself to say goodbye. With infinite relief she saw a cruising cab come along the boulevard towards them. She stepped off the pavement, waving her arm, and saw the cab veer her way. It pulled up beside her. She opened the door, then looked back over her shoulder. Niall was standing on the pavement in a pose she now recognised as characteristic of him: shoulders hunched, hands thrust in his pockets. She said in utter despair, 'We'll regret this for the rest of our lives, Niall,' and saw him take a step backwards, as though physically rejecting her words. She climbed in the cab, slammed the door, and gave her address in a choked voice. Then she leaned back in the seat and closed her eyes so she would not risk seeing him again. The blackness under her lids was the only refuge she had; she hugged her body with her arms and longed for the familiar surroundings of the apartment.

Magda was not home, would not be home for another hour. Nasturtium opened one eye, yawned, and shut it again. Joss kicked off her shoes at the door and prowled around the apartment, picking things up and putting them down again, all her movements as jerky and uncoordinated as a very small child's. Her throat was tight and her eyes burning, yet she was afraid to give in to tears for fear they might never stop. There was another reason. Niall knew her address. Perhaps, just perhaps, he would change his mind and follow her here and take her in his arms, and this unbearable, waking nightmare would be over.

But, although the minutes crept around the old-fashioned clock on the shelf, no one knocked on the door. One-twenty, one-thirty, one-forty . . . Magda would be home shortly after two. Joss knew she could not face Magda's bright-eyed curiosity at this time of the morning, so she went into her room, closed the door, undressed and got into bed. She was cold, her fingers as clammy as those of the dead. She lay very still, for if she moved too fast she might shatter into pieces, and stared up at the ceiling.

Some time later a key turned in the lock and Joss heard Magda speak to Nasturtium, who did not reply. For a few minutes Magda crept around the apartment, her exaggeratedly quiet movements striking on Joss's over-exposed nerves like hammer blows. Then the narrow line of light under Joss's door disappeared and Magda's bedroom door closed softly. The darkness was absolute.

Niall would not come now; it was too late. Joss clenched her teeth and felt the first tears seep from the corners of her eyes.

CHAPTER FIVE

THE digital clock on the dresser beside the bed said eleven minutes past ten. Joss rubbed her eyes, which were swollen from weeping, and looked again. The right-hand number had changed. Twelve minutes past ten. She had the feeling that a noise had woken her, dragging her upwards from a sodden sleep in which she had been dreaming. Or had the noise been part of her dream?

Twelve minutes past ten. Would Niall have left Toronto by now? She was quite sure that, for him, early in the morning would be before ten o'clock, and knew at the same time that she would not leave the apartment before noon, just in case he phoned. He knew Magda's last name; he could find the number in the book. She had meant to wake up early to be alert for the sound of the phone . . . she had no idea what time she had fallen asleep, although she remembered that the dawn light had been edging its way between the curtains.

She closed her eyes and tried to remember the beach near the farm, with the rock that was shaped like a charging buffalo, the curling lace of the waves, and the hissing of the eel grass in the onshore winds. But all she could see was the passionate hunger in Niall's blue eyes and all she could hear was his voice repudiating her, denying her the knowledge of even his name.

She could not bear her own thoughts. Pulling on her housecoat, Joss went out into the living-room. There was a note propped against the bowl of overripe bananas on the bamboo table, its gist that Magda had already left to spend the day with Charlie and would be home late tonight. So that was the noise that had awoken her.

Reading the note, Joss discovered that she now craved company, any company other than her own. She poured some of the very black coffee left in Magda's filter machine and looked at the clock on the shelf. Ten-seventeen. For the first Sunday that summer she wished it was a weekday so that she could go to work at the bookshop and then sing at the Red Lion. Even Mr Jodrey's company looked good today, she thought wretchedly. She picked up Saturday's newspaper and tried to read.

The telephone did not ring; not that Joss had really expected that it would. At noon she forced herself to eat something, then put on her jeans and went out. The sky had clouded over and there was a brisk wind, weather that she much preferred to the oppressive August heat. She began to walk and, whether consciously or unconsciously, her steps retraced all the places she had been with Niall: the newspaper stand where she had screamed his name in the rain; the crowded piers at the Harbourfront; the mellow brick facade of Scarlatti's; the wide boulevard of University Avenue. It was almost as though she hoped to conjure him up. He would appear among the Sunday afternoon strollers and take her arm, smiling at her with his blue eyes, and her world would be back on its axis.

She ate a salad at one of the pavement cafés, down by the water, trudged home, and fell asleep on the chesterfield cocooned in the pages of Saturday's paper, Nasturtium curled in the crook of her knees. At eight-thirty the telephone rang.

Joss leaped off the chesterfield. Nasturtium tumbled to the floor, her tail lashing with indignation; two pages of the entertainment section drifted down on top of her. Joss grabbed the receiver and croaked, *'Niall?'*

'Oh, dear, have I got the wrong number? I was sure I

dialled correctly, the trouble is there are so many numbers to remember. I'm terribly sorry to have bothered you.'

'Mum? It's OK, it's me, Joss.'

'Darling! You sound dreadful. Have you got a cold?'

Joss raked her fingers through her hair. 'No. I was asleep.'

'Why don't I call back later?'

'No, that's all right. How are you? And how's Dad?'

'Just fine.' Ellie MacDougall liked to talk, and the fact that a computer was charging her so much per minute for the privilege never discouraged her. She rambled on with assorted family news, which gave Joss the time to collect her wits. In the middle of a story about Gilbert's latest girlfriend Ellie suddenly said, 'Are you sure you're all right, Joss? You sound funny. Not quite all there.'

It was as good a description as any of Joss's emotional state. Wishing with all her heart that she could be transposed to the comfortable old couch in the kitchen of the farmhouse, she blurted, 'Mum, I met the right man—the one you always said I'd meet.'

Ellie prided herself on her liberated views. 'You mean he's there with you now—in bed? In that case, I *will* call back.'

'No, Mum, he's not!' Joss tried to steady her voice. 'I wish he were.'

'Begin at the beginning, dear. You're not making any sense.'

So Joss did, and found it a great relief to be able to speak about Niall openly. Ellie might talk a lot, but she also had the rarer capacity for being a good listener; putting in the occasional question, she heard her daughter's story from beginning to end. 'Very mysterious,' was her first comment. 'The most logical explanation is that he really is married.'

'If he is, then everything he said and did was a lie. I

can't believe that. I think he told me he was married just to get me off his back.'

'Maybe he's gay.'

'No, Mum.'

'Perhaps he's a famous politician who can't afford any romantic liaisons.'

'He told me he was a business executive. And if he was famous I'd have recognised him.'

'An undercover agent for narcotics or gunrunning. A spy. A member of the CIA. There could be all kinds of reasons why he didn't want to give you his name.'

'You've been reading too many of Gilbert's paperbacks.'

'Well, darling, if he was as truthful and as attracted to you as you say, there has to be a reason for his behaviour, doesn't there?'

Ellie's logic could never be disputed. 'Yes,' Joss said miserably. 'Maybe the simplest explanation is the real one. He really was married, and I was a fool to be taken in by him.'

'If he was unscrupulous enough to lie about his marital status, then he wouldn't have any trouble making up a false name. Besides which he would certainly have taken you to bed. Because you were, I gather, willing.'

'He felt so *right*,' Joss said in a whisper.

'Oh, dear. Then I really don't know what to say. Maybe he'll think it over and write to you.'

'Maybe the moon is made of green cheese.'

'*That* would please the dairy industry,' said Ellie. 'Darling, I wish you were nearer, I'm worried about you.'

'It's all so painful right now,' Joss gulped. 'It only happened yesterday. Surely in time I'll forget about him, or else decide he really wasn't the right man. Won't I?'

'The women in our family have a reputation for longevity in their love affairs,' Ellie said dishearteningly.

'Apart from my grandmother.'

'The exception who proves the rule. You'll be home in about three weeks, won't you, Joss?'

Home . . . Joss's throat closed in sudden longing. She swallowed hard and said, 'It depends what I do. I was offered a job at the research lab in Halifax, Mum, starting in October.'

'But what about medical school?' Ellie said in dismay.

'Medical school costs money.'

'But look how much you earn once you're finished. Why, Dr Hennigar just last week had a swimming pool and tennis courts built at his place. The pool was kidney-shaped. Rather bad taste, I thought.'

'I wouldn't earn a penny for six years, though.'

'Darling, you're only twenty-one. And medical school wouldn't give you much time to brood over this man.'

'Physician, heal thyself?' Joss said drily.

'You've got to admit that Dr Jocelyn MacDougall has a certain ring to it.'

Joss said curiously, 'You really want me to be a doctor, don't you?'

'You'd be underselling yourself to settle for a job in a lab. Both your father and I think you have a great deal to offer in a medical career.'

'Oh.' Joss swallowed again, touched. 'Well, I have about three days to decide, because I have to send my final deposit soon. Mum, this phone call is going to cost the entire month's milk bill.'

'Your father says the same thing every time I pick up the phone. Joss dear, take care of yourself. And call any time, you know I'm always here. We love you.'

'I love you, too. Thanks, Mum.' And Joss rang off.

Perhaps because she had been able to share her burden, she slept better that night. But Monday dragged by, for her whole psyche felt fractured. Either Niall was the man of integrity she had taken him for, in which case she was left with the riddle of his departure; or else he had deceived her from start to finish, which meant she could no longer trust her own judgement. Tired and heavy-eyed, Joss busied herself unpacking new shipments at the bookshop and arranging the books on the shelves; she had to force herself to enter the Red Lion at five o'clock, for a demon of hope had persuaded her that by some miracle Niall would be there waiting for her. He was not, of course. But the pub was full of memories, and she avoided every one of Cleo Laine's songs.

She got back to the apartment at nine-thirty, and stopped in the doorway in surprise. 'Magda! What are you doing home?'

Magda and Nasturtium were artistically arranged on the chesterfield, Madga in a long housecoat of unrelieved black that illuminated the creamy pallor of her skin. 'Stomach 'flu,' she said. 'Keep your distance.'

'Can I get you anything?'

'Nothing that bears any relationship to food.' Magda frowned at her friend. 'Looks to me as though you could be getting it too, Joss. You don't look so hot.'

Joss sat down heavily in the nearest chair, first removing Magda's knitting and a slithery pile of magazines. 'I wish all I had was stomach 'flu.'

Joss was not a complainer. Magda sat up a little straighter. 'I knew something was wrong.'

It seemed easier to talk about Niall the second time round. 'I met a man in the bar last Wednesday night,' Joss began.

'About time,' Magda announced. 'You've been living like a nun all summer.' She scratched Nasturtium between the ears. 'What did he look like?'

'Tall, dark hair, blue eyes,' said Joss, thinking even as she spoke what an inadequate description of Niall that was. Any number of men were tall and dark with blue eyes. 'Very good-looking,' she added, and went on with the story. But when she reached Thursday night, the night Niall had drunk so much, Magda, who had been listening intently, interrupted, 'Did he give his name?'

'Only his first name. Niall. Without an e.'

'Not his last name?'

'He never did tell me that.'

'Was he thin and kind of intense with a sprinkling of grey hair over his ears and an old-fashioned watch?' Magda asked with growing excitement. 'It looked expensive.'

'He was thin, yes. His watch was Swiss, with Roman numerals and a leather strap,' Joss said dazedly.

'Right on. And his eyes were the same colour as Charlie's car.'

Charlie's car was a very old Ford painted a lurid shade of azure. 'His eyes were a much nicer blue than Charlie's car,' Joss protested. 'They seemed to see right through you. But Magda, how do you know him?'

'He was at the club last Tuesday night. I was talking to him in one of my breaks.' Magda was encouraged to be friendly with the patrons, unlike Joss. Now Magda widened her eyes. 'No wonder you're depressed.'

'What do you mean?' Joss said slowly. 'I haven't told you what happened yet.'

'Goodness, Joss, it's terribly sad! He's so young.'

Wondering if perhaps Magda had a fever, Joss said, 'Are you delirious or something? I don't have any idea what you're talking about!'

'You mean he didn't tell you?'

'Tell me *what?*'

'That he's dying,' Magda said.

The clock ticked on the shelf. Nasturtium whimpered in her sleep, her whiskers twitching. *'Dying?'* Joss repeated blankly.

'Yes. Cancer, he said. The doctors have given him less

than a year.'

Aghast, Joss stared at her roommate, and the pieces of evidence fell into place in her brain one by one. Niall's leanness. Her initial impression of exhaustion. The so-called stitch he had taken when they were dancing. The curving red scar round his ribs. Even his peculiar reaction when she had mentioned the name of her roommate.

Strangely enough, in the midst of encroaching horror her first reaction was one of relief. Niall was the man of integrity she had thought him to be. She understood his reticence now, his refusal to give a last name that would allow her to trace him. She even understood his reaction to the story of Jake's dying wife. Nor had he lied to her: simply kept to himself an appalling secret. But then horror swamped that tiny pocket of reason and she pressed her hands to her face.

'Joss, don't look like that! You're scaring me.'

Though a pain that was actually physical, Joss managed to focus on Magda's distraught face. 'Why did he tell *you*?' she cried. 'He didn't tell me.'

'Because he knew he was never going to see me again,' Magda said forcefully. 'You look as though you're going to fall apart, Joss—go to the cupboard to the left of the sink right now and pour yourself a brandy. Go along.'

Lacking the will to resist, Joss did as she was told. Some of the brandy slopped on the counter because her hands were shaking so badly that the neck of the bottle rattled against the glass. She carried the glass back into the living-room and sat down again.

'Now drink it,' Magda ordered.

Obediently Joss swallowed a large mouthful of the brandy. It tasted as she had always imagined her father's paint stripper would taste, but it left a warm glow in the vicinity of her stomach. She said, and her voice was not overly friendly, 'Tell me exactly how you met him.'

'He came to the club late last Tuesday night. He was stone-cold sober and he only ordered one drink the whole time he was there. I couldn't figure out why he'd come—he seemed scarcely aware of his surroundings and he sure wasn't having a good time. But his eyes reminded me of Charlie's car and he was very good-looking, you've got to admit that—so in my break I sat down at his table and asked him what was wrong. He looked at me and said, "I'll never see you again in my life, will I?" So I said, "Not unless you come back to this club, you won't." "I won't do that," he said. "If I don't tell someone soon, I'll go crazy." Then he went on in the kind of voice you'd use to order another drink, "I had the prognosis confirmed today. Less than a year to live. A year from now the world will still be merrily spinning on its axis, but I won't be here to see it." '

Magda paused, her head to one side. 'We get a lot of weirdos in the club. But I knew right away this was for real. This guy meant every word he'd said. So I asked him if he had cancer and he said yes, and then I asked if he had any family. "A father I don't get along with," he said. "That's all. Just as well I never took the time to get married and have a couple of kids, isn't it? At least I get to face this thing on my own, with no one hanging on my coat-tails."

'I didn't like that attitude very much, so I said, "Families help out when you're ill." He laughed—a horrible laugh, like glass cracking—and said, "You couldn't be more wrong. I learned as a kid that each of us is alone. Separate. Disconnected. We live alone and we die alone." Then he finished his drink and said, "If I thought I'd ever see you again, I'd never have told you this. Thanks for listening."

'By then my break was over, and he left before the next one. On purpose, I'm sure—he didn't even look at me when he went out.'

Joss said quietly, 'I met him the very next night.'

'You're acting as though you fell head over heels in love with him,' Magda said astringently.

'I did. And I'm almost sure it was mutual.'

'Oh, lord,' said Magda. 'What did you do that for?'

'I didn't know he was ill—not that it would have made any difference.'

'You'd better tell me the whole story.'

Madga interrupted rather more than Ellie had, and Joss was more loquacious, not being under the constraints of long-distance; but eventually she finished her story. 'Do you know what my very last remark was?' she said miserably. ' "We'll regret this for the rest of our lives" ' . . . how could I have said that, Magda?'

'You didn't know.'

'He should have told me!'

'I can understand why he didn't.'

Joss had been looking for an ally. She gave her friend a suspicious stare. 'So tell me, if you're so smart.'

'Let's assume he fell in love with you—it sure sounds as though he did. What's he got to offer you, Joss? Marriage? That's a laugh! He'd be ill the whole time you were married and then you'd be a widow in less than a year. I think he did the right thing by pulling a disappearing act. In fact, I don't think he should even have got involved to the extent he did. Look at you—you're a wreck!'

'You're both wrong,' Joss said aggressively. 'If he'd told me, at least we could have been together. That's what life's all about. Sharing. Helping each other out. Being there.' She glared at Magda. 'If you go around looking for guarantees, you'll be safe, sure—but you won't have much of a life.'

'So he was noble but screwed up?'

'He was wrong,' Joss repeated stubbornly.

Magda gave Joss a long, considering look. 'Is there any way you can trace him?'

Joss hadn't even considered looking for Niall, all her thought processes having been submerged in a welter of emotion. 'I have a description that could fit dozens of men, a first name, and I know he caught a flight out of Toronto early this morning, but I don't know where to . . . it's hopeless. Magda.'

Magda threw aside the afghan that was over her legs and eased free of Nasturtium. 'I've got to go to the bathroom. Put the kettle on, Joss, and make some tea. We've got to think.'

Joss went into the kitchen, filled the kettle and put it on the stove. Then, as if a bullet had slammed into her chest, she bent almost double, pain searing every nerve-ending in her body. Niall was dying . . . *dying*.

Madga's voice seemed to come from a long way away. 'Joss, what's wrong?'

Blindly Joss turned into her friend's embrace and began to weep, harsh, tearing sobs that she was helpless to stop. She cried for a long time and came back to reality to find her nose jammed against Magda's collarbone. She pulled back. 'I've probably soaked your housecoat,' she quavered.

'It's drip-dry.'

'Thanks, Magda. I've been needing to do that for the last two days.'

'As you so aptly remarked, that's what life's all about—sharing,' Magda said flippantly. 'OK, kid, blow your nose, make the tea, and let's go in the living-room. We've got to plan a strategy.'

Belatedly Joss said, 'If you're not feeling well, this is the last thing you need.'

'Nothing like a real-life tragedy to put stomach' flu in its place. The tea, Joss.'

Joss said, sounding more like herself than she had all evening, 'It's a good thing Charlie's got a strong personality— you'd tromp all over him, otherwise.'

'Charlie is untrompable. That's one of the reasons

I'm marrying him,' Magda said smugly. 'The tea-bags are in the canister.'

Joss produced an approximation of a laugh and made the tea. When she and Magda were settled in the living-room Magda said briskly, 'The first thing you have to decide is whether you do want to trace this man. He doesn't want to be traced. And after all, you only knew him for four days.'

Without hesitation Joss said, 'I have to try, Magda. He's the right man for me, and if we've only got a year there's no time to waste.'

Madga raised expressive brows and said, 'OK. You can check the ticket agents at the airport, and the hospitals. And that cab driver would probably remember him.'

'The two restaurants we went to—he made a reservation at each one.'

'Now you're talking. I'll check at the club—he might have paid his bill with a charge card.'

'I can do the same thing at the Red Lion.' Joss crinkled her brows. 'I can't think of anything else.'

'Out of all that we'll surely get his last name.' Magda raised her mug. 'To the search!'

Joss drank the toast in brandy, feeling it might be more efficacious, and shortly afterwards went to bed. She felt almost peaceful after her storm of crying, and full of hope. She would find Niall because he and she were meant to be together for whatever time he had left. She was clinging to this thought when she fell asleep, and it was still with her in the morning.

At the bookshop on Tuesday Joss arranged to have the next day off. She would lose a day's pay, but that couldn't be helped. At four she ran all the way to the little Italian restaurant where she and Niall had eaten last Friday, and asked the *maître d'* if she could see the reservation list for that day. He gave her sweat-streaked face a quizzical look, but produced his book obligingly enough. 'Nine-thirty on Friday, you say? Only three names, madam. Brooks, Diamond and Bernardi.'

'Diamond?' she repeated weakly.

'Yes. His second visit . . . although he didn't have a reservation the first time. A tall, dark-haired gentleman. In fact, you were with him, were you not, madam?'

Quailing at the thought of explanations, Joss gasped, 'Yes. Thank you for your help,' and left the restaurant with as much dignity as she could muster. Once outside she began running again, trying to rid herself of a crushing disappointment. She made it to her stool in the pub by one minute to five, and started with a couple of guitar solos so she could catch her breath.

In her break she phoned Scarlatti's. Although the list of names was considerably longer, among them was the name Diamond. Neither of the other names from the Italian restaurant was repeated. Joss hung up, biting her lip. She had had high hopes of the reservation list.

At nine o'clock Joss approached the cashier at the front desk of the Swansea. Her name was Helen, and she was from Nova Scotia. Cheerfully she went through all the credit card receipts from the Red Lion for the four nights Niall had been there. Although two men with the first name Neil had paid by credit card, both spelled their name with an e, and both had been guests at the hotel. Another dead end.

On Wednesday Joss spend a harrowing two hours at the Toronto hospital that was renowned for its cancer treatment. The number of departments and the proliferation of specialists were mind-boggling, and she spoke to at least a dozen receptionists, who ranged from pleasant to rude. The last was the worst. She was a sharp-nosed woman in her forties with thin lips, who used a minimum of words. After Joss had described Niall and given the probable dates, the woman said officiously, 'The patient's last name?'

'I don't know it—I explained that to you.'

'I cannot access the computer without a surname.'

'I'm not asking the computer,' Joss said as politely as she could. 'I'm asking you if you remember him.'

'I see something like a hundred patients a day. I could not possibly remember them all. Now if you'll excuse me, I have work to do.' She turned away, giving Joss a view of the back of her head, where her hair was scraped into a stingy little bun. Joss left.

She took a bus to the airport. More line-ups, this time blanked-face travellers surrounded by mounds of luggage, old people in wheelchairs, children squalling. By dint of making enquiries, Joss succeeded in leaving notices posted in various staff rooms; she did not know what else to do.

Her last stop was the dingy office of the cab company. Two-way radios crackled and barked; the walls were plastered with city maps interspersed with graffiti. Joss gave the registration number of the cab to one of the controllers, who told her the cabbie would be checking in during the next hour. Joss sat down on a wooden bench to wait.

One of the controllers had smoked eleven cigarettes, and the other, six, before rescue came in the form of a remembered voice speaking over the intercom. 'Herb?' said the older woman, lighting her twelfth cigarette from the butt of the eleventh. 'Lady at the office wants to see you, c'n you drop by on your way?'

'Sure thing,' squawked Herb. 'Gimme five minutes.'

Joss smiled her thanks and went outdoors to wait. A yellow cab pulled up by the kerb a couple of minutes later and Herb got out. He saw Joss, clapped a hand dramatically to his forehead and said, 'Don't tell me! I bin readin' this book about developin' your memory. Wait, now . . . I got it. The guy who nearly got run over and then left you standin' in the rain. Boy, did I tell him a thing or two. Listen, mister, I said to him, that gal saved your life and you didn't even say thanks. Serve you right if she didn't bother next time, just let you get run over deader 'n a doornail——'

Joss covered her ears. She was not convinced she had saved Niall's life, but if she had, her action must have seemed ironic, to say the least. 'Here's another test for your memory,' she said quickly. 'Did he tell you his name? And where did you take him?'

'Lady, you're not still chasin' that guy? He ain't worth it. Lots more where he came from.'

Joss clasped her hands, looked piteous and said with the utmost sincerity, 'It's *very* important that I find him.'

Herb shook his head. 'My old man always used to tell me it's a waste of time tryin' to figure out what goes on between a broad's ears. Blamed it on the moon, he did, all them——'

'Herb!' Joss said loudly. 'Where did you take him?'

'OK, OK, I was gettin' there. No, he didn't tell me his name. Didn't tell me anythin', come right down to it. Guess he didn't appreciate what I had to say.' Joss looked about ready to burst. 'I let him off at the corner of St Clair and Yonge,' Herb finished hurriedly.

'You mean he didn't ask for a particular place—a hotel or an apartment block?'

'Nope. Corner of St Clair and Yonge. Out he got and walked off into the rain. I sure didn't try to follow him . . . why should I?'

Yet another dead end. 'Did he tip you?' Joss asked.

'Paid his fare and split. Would you tip someone who read you a lecture?'

'I guess not.' She took a bill out of her purse. 'Thanks for talking to me, Herb.'

'Any time—sorry I couldn't help you. You take my advice and forget that guy.' Herb leaped back into his cab and took off down the street. Joss began walking in the direction of the Red Lion, and when she related her lack of results to Magda the next morning was given advice very similar to Herb's.

'He paid cash at the pub as well,' Magda said. 'So your only hope is that someone at the airport will remember him.' She went on earnestly, 'You've done all you can, Joss. Let sleeping dogs lie and get on with your life. Sure, it's painful right now, but you'll forget him in time, I know you will.'

Ellie used much the same words on her next phone call. 'Forget him, darling. It's not easy, but I think you must. After a while he'll seem like a dream you had, you'll see.'

Joss did not believe any of these well-meaning sentiments. Niall was still achingly real to her, his dreadful predicament weighing on her mind night and day, his absence as keenly felt as an amputation. However, because of him, the decision about her future was easily solved. She would become a doctor so she could help people like him; and she would go to the university that was only a hundred miles from Toronto on the off-chance that somehow she would meet him again. She sent off her deposit and on the first of September took the train home to Nova Scotia for a five-day break before classes began.

Her family and the old clapboard farmhouse enfolded her in their arms. The sweetbriar roses were still in bloom, and Bert the collie stirred himself to lick her hand. Ellie, after one look at her daughter's strained features, cooked all Joss's favourite meals, while George enlisted her help in bringing in the final hay crop of the season. Joss had always loved haying, and now the hard physical labour coupled with day-long doses of country air helped her to sleep.

On her last evening home she and Ellie walked to the orchard together. Joss looked up the slope between the straight rows of trees. No blossoms, no dandelions, no blue-eyed stranger stepping out into the clearing. 'This is where I always pictured myself meeting the man of my dreams, Mum,' she confessed. 'How's that for teenage fantasy? Me in a white dress, him bathed in sunlight, violins playing in the distance.' Her smile was twisted. 'Didn't quite work out that way, did it?'

'Real life can be very cruel,' Ellie said soberly.

'If he cared for me at all, I still can't understand why he didn't tell me,' Joss cried.

'He did what he felt was best. That's all any of us can do.'

In a low voice Joss said, 'Do you know what the worst part of all this is? I'll never know what happened to him.'

Ellie put her arm around her daughter's waist. 'Darling, anything I can say sounds like a cliché. But time does heal, and we do learn to love again. You have so much of life ahead of you—in time Niall will take his proper place in your memory and you'll find someone else to love.'

Joss bowed her head. On the branch brushing her sleeve hung half a dozen slowly ripening apples: the blossom had borne fruit. But in her case frost had touched the flowers and the tree was barren. Her mother was wrong, she thought dully. Niall had her heart. In a strange way he always had; and he always would.

CHAPTER SIX

Dr Jocelyn Eleanor Macdougall, MD, Speciality in Family Medicine, regarded herself in the mirror with a certain satisfaction. Today she and her two partners had signed a one-year lease for the building on Queen Street West where they planned to open a clinic; renovations were to start at eight o'clock tomorrow morning. Three weeks, said the contractor. Joss was counting on at least a month. Either way, by June of this year she would be beginning the practice of medicine, the goal for which she had worked so hard the last six years. While her accumulated student loans were astronomical, and while she had reached the remarkable age of twenty-seven on her last birthday, she was well content with the path her life had taken. She loved medicine. She had thrown herself into her studies all those years ago, sparing nothing, and had been rewarded with the surety of a vocation.

She leaned forward and began swiftly applying her make-up; last year during her internship she had learned to do many things in the least possible time. Bryan was taking her out for dinner. Bryan in theory espoused punctuality, which meant in practice that if a problem arose in his research he would be late, but that if he were on time he thoroughly disliked having to wait for anyone else. Joss had threatened him with dire consequences were he to be late for their wedding, due to take place two weeks from Saturday. He had given his rare laugh, which she liked so much, and had told her Dr Michaud would be taking over the research progamme for a whole week; he, Bryan, would be waiting for her at the altar.

She smoothed green eye-shadow over her lids and outlined the lower edge with a pencil. Dr Bryan MacFarlane worked for the Hospital for Sick Children in Toronto; Joss had met him when he had given a number of lectures in paediatrics to the fouth-year medical students at Western. His courtship had beeen slow and deliberate, which had suited her fine, giving her time to appreciate the brilliance of his mind and his dedication to his job, as well as to be secretly amused by the conventionality of his morals. She had never made love with Bryan, for he had made it very clear that he wished to wait until the fourth finger on her left hand was encircled by the expensive platinum and diamond wedding band that he had chosen for her. Although she rarely admitted this to herself openly, she knew in the secret recesses of her mind that a large part of Bryan's attraction was the difference between him and Niall.

Joss uncapped her mascara and remembered, as she almost always did, the dollar-forty-nine lashes. She had never forgotten Niall, although now she could remember him without pain, as a brief, intensely meaningful espisode of her life that had changed her irrevocably. Because of Niall she had learned about helplessness in the hands of fate and about the pangs of grief, and she knew that these hard-won lessons had made her more understanding with her patients, more sympathetic and more tolerant.

The first year after she had met Niall had been the worst, for, with her during her lectures and labs and hours of study, she had carried the knowledge that his illness must be progressing. She had been sure she would know intuitively the moment of his death, and had discovered as the months passed that even that was denied her; she had never received any sense that Niall was no longer on this earth. She had kept very much to herself her first two years at medical school, but during her third year had tentatively started to date a little. Bryan had been good for her, never rushing her or applying undue pressure, apparently content with the warmth and steady affection she gave him. She could not give him passion or the fierce flame of a love that brooks no denial, for those had been Niall's and seemed to have been snuffed out over the slow, agonising months of that first year.

Joss recapped her mascara, applied a coral lipstick and inserted the gold filigree ear-rings that had been Bryan's graduation gift to her. Then she ran a brush through her hair; it was the same streaked, tawny blonde that it had been six years ago, although she had had it cut during her second year—the year in which there was the highest percentage of drop-outs from medical school—because there simply had not been the time to spend drying its long, thick waves. She now wore it feathered about her head with her ears bare, a style that gave more prominence to her gold-flecked eyes and to the new maturity of her features.

Quickly she stood up. Her green, Chanel-styled suit, a Christmas gift from her parents, was hanging in the wardrobe. She slipped it on, added elegant taupe pumps that she had bought with her first pay cheque, and checked her appearance in the mirror again.

The mirror reflected a beautiful and assured young woman, warm, approachable, yet with a sense of inner depths that would be accessible to very few. Joss did not see any of this. She adjusted a shoulder pad in her jacket and the neckline of her cream-coloured blouse and decided she would do.

The doorbell rang. Bryan was exactly on time. She opened the door and said, 'The tissue cultures must have behaved themselves today.'

'All very well for you to talk—you're a lady of leisure.'

She laughed; when she had finished interning two weeks ago, she had flown home and lazed on the farm for ten blissful days. 'Tomorrow I start bugging the contractors,' she said.

'And reading up on measles and mumps,' Bryan said drily.

She led him into the kitchen and poured him a drink.

'You don't really approve of the clinic, do you?'

'I'd rather see you specialise; it's the only way to get ahead. Paediatrics, for instance.'

'Practised out of an elegant suite in Rosedale.'

He raised his glass. 'You know I'm being honest with you, Joss, when I say I worry about the neighbourhood you've chosen. Pretty rough, and they won't all see you as an angel of mercy.'

'But you're taking me out to dinner to celebrate signing the lease,' she said provocatively.

'If I've learned one thing since I met you, it's that you're going to do what you're going to do. I want you to know my opinion—but I won't try to stop you.'

'Freedom,' Joss said thoughtfully.

'Very important.'

So it was. But she would have preferred Bryan to have endorsed her plans for a family clinic in a poor area of town. She said lightly, 'We could take our drinks in the living-room.'

'I've been sitting all day. I had to do statisical analyses on the last batch of reports.' He began describing the results, his voice as animated as it ever got. A lot of Bryan's research concerned burn victims, and in practical terms his long hours in the laboratory had resulted in less pain, less danger of infection and more comfort for the patients. Joss knew this, so her interest in and respect for his work were genuine.

They finished their drinks and Bryan checked his watch. 'We should leave.'

'Where are we going?'

'Scarlatti's . . . I know you like it there.'

The first time Bryan had taken her to Scarletti's, nearly two years ago, had been the first time Joss had been back since the evening she had spent there with Niall. She had found that second visit unexpectedly painful. The strong resurgence of memories had taken her aback; their clarity and immediacy had frightened her. She had said nothing of this to Bryan, for she had not known him particularly well then; and somehow the occasion had never arisen since then for her to talk about Niall. Those four days had been so brief and ephemeral an experience, so deeply felt yet ending so inconclusively, that she had shrunk from exposing them to a man as rational and pragmatic as Bryan. Anyway, Niall was gone. What was the use of talking about him?

Now she joked, 'It's their chocolate decadence dessert that I like!'

'You don't have to worry about your figure, Joss.'

She said a touch tartly, 'I'm never sure that you even notice my figure.'

'Oh, I do. Don't you worry about that.'

'You're a dark horse, Bryan MacFarlane.'

'They're the ones who often win the race, Joss.'

She gave him a sudden gamine grin, because it was exchanges like this that convinced her their marriage would work out. She said, 'You look very smart this evening yourself, sir.'

Bryan, at six feet, looked taller because he held himself so straight. His brown hair had a military cut, while his grey eyes were his most expressive feature in a face that was conventionally good-looking. He rarely bought off-the-rack clothing and he disliked leisure pursuits that involved getting dirty. He had visited the farm with Joss and, while he had been polite, he had not fitted in; Joss had seen him surreptitiously removing Bert's hairs from his creased grey flannels and eyeing the manure pile with fastidious distaste. George had been puzzled by him, and Ellie a little over-friendly. Jake had said bluntly, 'He's the wrong man, sis,' and had walked away before she could argue. The wedding was to be held in St David's Church in Toronto, the reception at Bryan's mother's house. Of Joss's family, only her parents were attending.

As they left the apartment, Joss carrying her spring coat because she knew the air would be cold later on, she began chattering about wedding plans. Although originally she had wanted a small, intimate wedding, the list of guests Bryan had given her had precluded any notions of intimacy; she had, however, chosen a very beautiful white silk suit instead of a full-length gown, and had dissuaded Bryan from an engagement ring. 'I'd rather we spend the money on a trip,' she had said.

'Joss, I earn enough that we can do both. I'd like to buy you a diamond.'

'A great big diamond ring would look totally out of place at the clinic,' Joss had argued. 'Besides, someone might bop me over the head to steal it.'

'That's exactly what I dislike about that clinic,' Bryan had said touchily. But to Joss's relief the discussion about an engagement ring had never been reopened.

It was May now, and the city's trees were unfurling fresh green leaves. Bryan parked near the restaurant. He locked his car, a black BMW, and he and Joss walked towards the brick steps of Scarlatti's. The restaurant's tiny walled garden had pollarded cherry trees in fragrant bloom, white as a bridal wreath. City version of an orchard, Joss thought wryly. The orchard at home would only be in bud now.

Restrained elegance was the keynote of Scarlatti's foyer. The carpet was plum-coloured and the lighting discreet; crimson roses glowed in an oak-panelled alcove. The *maître d'*, whose name was Rupert, recognised Bryan immediately, for Bryan and his colleagues were regular customers. 'Good evening, Dr MacFarlane. Madame, may I take your coat? The evenings are still cool, aren't they?'

Joss passed over her coat. 'Your trees are very pretty, Rupert,' she said politely.

'Thank you, madam. They are enjoying their brief moment of glory,' Rupert replied with a grandiloquence that Joss had come to expect from him; it went with his waxed moustache and the flourish with which he hung up her coat, rather as if he were a bullfighter and it the red cape.

Behind him the leaded-glass door of the restaurant opened again. 'Ah, good evening, sir,' Rupert said with something approaching genuine warmth. 'How nice to see you again.'

Joss half turned to see who the gentleman was who had elicited so much enthusiasm from Rupert. A couple had entered the door, the woman ahead of the man. She was a striking, patrician-faced blonde whose fur jacket would have paid off at least a year of Joss's student loan. Then the man stepped into the pool of light cast by the crystal chandelier and Joss dropped her bag. Her whole body went ice-cold with primitive terror. Her ears roared. I'm dreaming, she thought, panic-stricken. This isn't happening. It can't happen.

The man who was standing in the foyer was Niall.

She must have made a tiny, choked sound. His eyes, the blue eyes that she had never forgotten, swivelled round to look at her. She watched the colour drain from his face and from a distance that seemed immeasurable heard his shocked whisper, *'Joss . . .'*

'N-Niall?' she stammered.

'My God—Joss!'

He took a step towards her; she could not have moved to have saved her soul. 'You died,' she croaked. 'Five years ago.'

Rupert said reprovingly, for this was a scene and Scarlatti's did not favour scenes, 'Mr Morgan is a regular customer, madam. May I please show you to your table?'

Bryan said impatiently, 'Come along, Joss,' and the patrician blonde looked down her elegant nose.

Joss wanted to scream at them all to go away, for this scene was between herself and Niall, and no one else mattered. Striving for some kind of normality, she faltered, 'Bryan, I'd like you to meet a—an acquaintance of mine. Niall——' She stopped in consternation. What name had Rupert given him?

Smoothly Niall filled the gap. 'Niall Morgan,' he said, stepping forwards and holding out his hand.

Short of outright rudeness, Bryan had to take the proffered hand. 'Bryan MacFarlane,' he said in a chilly voice.

Niall put a hand on the blonde's elbow. 'My friend, Trilby Henderson-Smythe.'

Joss was shot through by a red-hot jealousy from Niall's most casual of gestures. The blonde *would* have a name like that, she thought meanly, and tried to produce a smile from lips that seemed to have congealed on her face. 'I'm pleased to meet you,' she said mechanically.

With a great aplomb Bryan said, 'Good evening, Miss Henderson-Smythe.' The blonde favoured him with a smile that could have graced the pages of *Vanity Fair*. Joss and Niall said nothing. Joss was afraid to look at Niall for fear he might have disappeared again; the only way to convince herself that he was flesh and blood was to touch him, and that she could not bring herself to do. Then Bryan put a proprietorial arm around her shoulders and said heartily, 'Very nice to have met you both. I hope you'll enjoy your meal here as much as we always do—you have quite a reputation to live up to, Rupert.'

'Indeed, sir,' Rupert said suavely, and took two leather-bound menus and a wine list from the glossy mahogany buffet. 'Please come this way, Dr MacFarlane.'

Joss shot one last desperate glance over her shoulder. Niall was still standing by the blonde. He had not disappeared. In a sudden surge of emotion that filled her eyes with tears she said clearly, 'I'm so glad you're alive, Niall.' Then she automatically followed in Rupert's wake.

The spiral staircase was ablaze with scarlet and orange tulips, fringed and fluted. Daffodils nodded around the fountain. Rupert led them to their regular table, seated Joss with much ceremony and passed her the menu, which was as heavy as a book. He shook out her serviette and placed it on her lap. She had never realised before how much that gesture irritated her.

Bryan said politely, 'Your usual, Joss?' She nodded, and he ordered a Martini and a Manhattan. Then he opened the menu.

Joss's back was to the entrance. But by the prickling of hair on the back of her neck she knew when Niall came into the room. Fortunately the tables immediately surrounding them were all filled, for she did not think she could have borne to have had him sitting too near to her. She sneaked a surreptitious glance over her shoulder. He and the blonde were being escorted to a table near the fountain; by turning her head only slightly she had a perfect view of them. Niall was facing her.

Because she was still not convinced that this was not a dream, Joss put her hands in lap and pinched her wrist, hard. It hurt, nor did she wake up to find herself in bed in her apartment with its west-facing windows that never admitted the morning sun. She was awake. This was real. Niall was not dead.

He was very much alive, she thought with a constriction in her chest. Alive and something like sixty feet away from her, sitting with an extremely beautiful woman who also looked—Joss had to be fair—intelligent. The woman was not his wife, at least she had that much to be grateful for.

'You haven't even looked at the menu,' Bryan said.

She started nervously, looking at her companion with a puzzled frown, as if wondering who he was. 'Pardon me?'

He added grimly, 'Let's get dinner ordered and then we can talk.'

Everything in order and under control, Joss thought with a touch of hysteria. She did not feel the slightest bit hungry, and the mere thought of chocolate decadence made her feel ill. She opened the menu, quickly picked out a garden salad and sole *bonne femme* and closed it again. Niall was looking at the menu; even at this distance she could see that he was frowning. Then the waiter interposed his starched white shirt and green satin cummerbund between her and Niall. She gave her order. After asking for mussels *à la provencale* and prime rib of beef *au jus,* Bryan began to discuss the choice of wines with the waiter. Joss did not contribute to the discussion; she did not even feel capable of deciding between white and red.

When the waiter went away, Niall and Trilby Henderson-Smythe reappeared. Bryan said testily, 'I wish you'd stop staring at that chap. Who is he, anyway?'

She took a healthy swallow of her Martini, and its bite jolted her back to awareness. 'I knew him very briefly six years ago,' she said, looking straight into Bryan's level grey eyes. 'Then he simply . . . disappeared. I found out afterwards that he had terminal cancer. So naturally I'd presumed him dead. It—it was like seeing a ghost to meet him again.' She ran out of words and fished the olives out of her Martini, chewing them thoroughly.

'Did you have an affair with him?'

She looked up, surprised. Bryan was not normally intuitive; she must have looked ghastly at that first sight of Niall. 'I've never had an affair with anyone, Bryan, I told you that,' she said slowly.

'I thought you were going to faint when you saw him.'

She said carefully, 'Even though I only knew him for a short time, I was very attracted to him. So it was a shock to see him again.'

'Particularly as he had never done you the courtesy of letting you know he survived.' Bryan only used that clipped voice when he was angry.

'He wouldn't have known where to find me, I suppose.'

'So are any other skeletons going to emerge from your closet before we get married, Joss?'

His tone was joking, his eyes were not. 'Maybe I should have told you about Niall,' Joss said. 'But I was convinced the man was dead years before I met you, Bryan. The whole episode was over. Dead. Gone. Buried.'

'You sound very vehement.' Bryan stabbed at his drink with the cocktail stick.

Recklessly she took another large gulp of her Martini. 'Are we having a fight? You're the last man in the world I would have suspected of jealousy.'

'I wouldn't have suspected myself of it, either. But there was something about the way the two of you looked at each other . . .' He shrugged his shoulders irritably. 'I sure didn't like it.'

'Neither did Rupert,' Joss answered, trying to lighten the atmosphere between them.

'Rupert does not care for unbridled emotion. He thinks eating at Scarlatti's is the acme of civilised behaviour.'

She had to laugh. 'Don't ever tell him that it's not.'

Bryan suddenly reached across the table, took her hand in his and said, 'I love you, Joss. I want to marry you.'

Bryan only rarely verbalised his feelings. Feeling as farouche as if Niall was standing behind her chair listening to every word, Joss said weakly, 'We *are* getting married. In just over two weeks, in case you'd forgotten.'

'I wish it was tomorrow,' Bryan said forcefully.

She, Joss discovered with a sinking of her heart, was glad it was not. But how could she say that to Bryan? She discovered within herself a strong craving to be alone. All by herself in her apartment, so that she could sit quietly and assimilate the astounding knowledge that Niall was alive.

But she was not alone. Bryan was sitting across from her with an expectant look on his face: clearly he wanted an answer. She had no idea what to say. 'I'm sorry I'm behaving so peculiarly,' she managed. 'For a moment I really did think I was seeing a ghost. We all make light of ghost stories, don't we? We tell them around the campfire and then we creep off to bed looking back over our shoulders. Haunted houses and nervous giggles . . . it's not funny at all when you really are convinced you're seeing a ghost. I was terrified.'

'Will you see this Niall Morgan again?' Bryan demanded.

Joss looked at him blankly. She had scarcely taken in
that Niall was alive; she had not even thought about seeing
him again. 'I don't know where he lives, what he does . . .
I don't know anything about him.'

'You're not answering the question, Joss.'

'It's not the right question!'

'I would have thought it a very pertinent question. All
things considered.'

Dimly, she supposed he was right. She shot a hunted
glance at the table near the fountain. Niall was staring at
her. Her eyes skidded away.

With a timing for which she could feel nothing but
gratitude, the waiter's cummerbund blocked her view of
the fountain. A green salad was put in front of her. Bryan
was given an array of mussels broiled on the half-shell,
pungent with garlic. Quickly Joss picked up her knife and
fork and began to eat. Bryan, she knew, was still waiting
for an answer and was obstinate enough to be silent until
she produced one. Two can play that game, she thought,
and buttered a slice of Scarlatti's warm herb bread.

Bryan was the first to speak, although not until their
appetisers had been removed and they were waiting for the
main course. 'I can see you're not going to answer me,' he
said coldly.

'I can't. I don't know what to say. Bryan, can't we talk
about the deficit or the effects of viral hepatitis? Please.'

'It's unlike you to be anything but straightforward,' was
his pompous reply.

'I'm sorry!' Joss cried in exasperation, looking anything
but sorry. Then they sat in strained silence until the arrival
of the sole and the beef *au jus*. Joss bolted her food, which
would have further upset Rupert, her one desire to be gone
from Scarlatti's and never to come back. She had cleaned
her plate before Bryan was even half-way through his
meal. She picked up her bag, said, 'Excuse me, please,'
and headed for the cloakroom.

The anteroom of the ladies had the same plum-coloured

carpeting as the foyer, chairs vaguely reminiscent of the eighteenth-century French style, and two artistic floral arrangements. Joss liked her flowers natural, not with wires stuck in their stems. She sat down and found herself once more staring at her own reflection in a mirror. She repaired her lipstick, fluffed up her hair and adjusted the neckline of her blouse again; it had never lain quite straight. She should have returned the blouse right after she had worn it for the first time, but she had been interning in obstetrics then, running short on sleep, and returning a blouse had been low on her priority list . . . oh, God, what was she going to do?

Niall was alive. He had not died, after all.

She found herself repeating those two sentences over and over again, as if repeating them would somehow make sense of them. It did not seem to.

Another woman came in, gave Joss a curious look, and went through to the other room. Joss stood up. Much as she might like to, she could not hide in the woman's room for ever. She pushed open the door and stepped outside.

Niall was standing in the dimly lit corridor, a situation so reminiscent of the Red Lion that Joss felt a thrill of superstitious terror. 'What are you doing here?' she cried, and by 'here' could have meant here on earth or here outside the Ladies.

Niall grabbed her by the sleeve, as if he was afraid she might turn and run. 'I had to talk to you,' he said hoarsely.

She looked down. His hand was just as she remembered it, the long, lean fingers, the sprinkle of dark hair. Overcome by an emotion she could not have defined, she suddenly leaned her forehead on his shoulder, the nape of her neck a vulnerable curve. 'I can't believe you're alive,' she whispered helplessly, and felt his other arm go around her and hold her as if the past six years had never happened.

'How did you know I was ill?' he asked. 'I never told

you.'

'Magda.'

'One of life's little coincidences that you happened to be rooming with the one woman in Toronto to whom I'd told the truth,' he said caustically.

'Not really a coincidence. The club was near the hotel, and she's the one who got me the job at the Red Lion. Niall, why are we standing here talking about Magda?'

His arm tightened. 'I've got to see you again.'

'I don't know whether——'

'Joss, I've *got* to! To have found you after all these years . . .'

She raised her head, her eyes blazing. 'It was your choice to lose me in the first place.'

'I know, I know. I did what I thought was best.'

'I don't think it——'

'Look, we can't get into that now. Give me your phone number and I'll call you first thing tomorrow morning.' Niall's face changed. 'God, Joss, you're more beautiful than you ever were.'

The other woman emerged from the cloakroom just as he spoke, and gave Joss an even more curious look. Joss said inanely, 'I'm going out at ten o'clock.'

'Then I'll call at nine-thirty. Please, Joss.' He gave her a crooked smile, his eyes very blue. 'Don't take all evening to decide . . . when I left the restaurant the gentleman at your table was looking rather fussed.'

Niall had given her the perfect opportunity to say that the gentleman at her table was her fiancé. Joss said nothing. Opening her handbag with fingers that shook, she found a notepad and a pen, wrote her phone number on the pad and tore off the piece of paper. For a moment she held it in her hand, knowing that by giving it to him she was doing something momentous, the consequences of which could disrupt her life.

Perhaps Niall sensed this. He loosened her grip on the paper and took it from her, first folding it carefully then putting it in the inner pocket of his suit jacket. 'Nine-thirty,' he said. 'Now you'd better go back to your table—it would hardly do for your gentleman-friend to pursue us to the cloakroom.'

'How can you manage to joke about this?' she muttered.

'Joss, if I didn't keep this conversation on some kind of even keel I'd be throwing you on the floor and making love to you.'

'Oh,' she gulped. 'Oh, I see.' She added idiotically, 'Rupert would not approve.'

'Nor would Bryan MacFarlane or Trilby. Off you go, I'll follow in a minute.'

Joss made a groping gesture with one hand, dropped it to her side in frustration, and said with desperate honesty, 'You promise you'll phone? You won't just disappear again?'

'I promise.'

He was a man who kept his promises. She turned away, a simple physical movement that seemed to take a huge effort of will, and hurried down the corridor to the restaurant. Bryan was sitting exactly where she had left him. He looked thunderous. She slid into her seat; the dinner plates had been removed.

'Did you enjoy that little tête-à-tête?' Bryan said nastily. 'Which cloakroom did you choose—the men's or the women's?'

Joss felt anger flood her veins. 'Bryan, I did not plan that little tête-à-tête, as you call it. Niall and I only talked for a minute or two. But he's going to call me tomorrow morning.'

Bryan had obviously not expected such frankness. 'I trust you told him that you and I are engaged.'

Her eyes fell. 'I didn't, no. I will tomorrow.'

'I'd appreciate that,' he said sarcastically. Then with a complete change of voice he said to the waiter, 'Ah, thank you . . . yes, that one goes to the lady.'

The waiter put a dessert glass in front of Joss; it contained chocolate ice-cream, chocolate mousse and chocolate sauce. She looked at it with concealed loathing, and heard Bryan say, 'I knew you'd want chocolate decadence.'

'Thank you,' she said, knowing he had meant well and knowing she must make an effort to eat it. From the corner of her eye she saw Niall edge through the tables near the fountain, and forced herself not to stare. She took a large spoonful of the mousse, which was laced with rum, and said valiantly, 'Wonderful.'

The waiter brought coffee, cream and demerara sugar. While Joss plugged away at the chocolate decadence, Bryan began to discuss the common stocks he had sold the day before at an excellent profit margin. Joss tried to listen intelligently, recognising the conversation as an oblique attempt at reconciliation, wishing that chocolate had never been invented. When she finished the dessert Bryan lit a cigar, something he called his only vice. He smoked it with agonising slowness.

The waiter brought the bill, discreetly encased in a leather folder; Bryan inserted his credit card into the folder and the waiter bore them both away. Normally Joss would have split the bill with him, but tonight was Bryan's treat, to celebrate the lease on the clinic. Which had not, she realised, been mentioned since they had left the apartment. Her ten-thirty appointment the next day was with the contractor.

Finally they were ready to leave. Bryan stood up and pulled her chair out for her. She also stood up. For a split second she looked towards the fountain. Niall was watching her. She dropped her eyes and walked steadily out of the restaurant, remembering to nod at the waiter, then making polite small talk with Rupert in the foyer. Yes, the dinner had been excellent, as usual; yes, she would put on her coat. The air would be cold after being indoors; thank you so much, goodnight, goodnight.

Joss had never been so glad to leave a restaurant in her whole life. Once seated in the car, she leaned her head back and closed her eyes. Bryan accompanied her up to the apartment as he always did, and, although she would infinitely have preferred to be alone, she let him follow her inside without comment. He hung up her coat, then said punctiliously, 'I'm not going to stay long, Joss—early day at the lab tomorrow. But I do want to say that I'm sorry about tonight. I over-reacted, I know. I hope you'll forgive me.'

He was standing ramrod-straight and made no attempt to touch her. He also looked reassuringly real; Bryan would never disappear as Niall had. In swift compunction Joss said, 'Of course you're forgiven. *I* over-reacted, too. But to see someone walking around whom you'd believed dead is an awful shock, and one for which I had no preparation whatsoever.'

'I hope he will call tomorrow. It might be as well for the two of you to get together—for explanations, if nothing else.' Bryan cleared his throat and added awkwardly, but with great sincerity, 'I have every faith in you, Joss. I know you'll handle the situation well, and I know you'll never deceive me.'

She was touched by these sentiments. Very naturally she moved into his embrace, something she would not have thought possible five minutes ago. 'Thank you for being so understanding, Bryan.'

He kissed her firmly on the lips, then moved back. 'Something I neglected to do this evening was to wish your clinic every success, Joss. You're excited about it, aren't you? You'll do a great job, I'm sure.'

'I'm as excited about it as a kid at Christmas,' she confessed. 'I wish we could move into the building right away.'

'Put a bomb under the contractor tomorrow,' Bryan said in his staid voice.

Her eyes twinkled. 'I'll do my best. Thanks for dinner,

Bryan. I didn't thank you properly at the time.'

'My pleasure.' He kissed her once more. 'I'll see you tomorrow. We're having dinner with my mother at seven, remember?'

Joss locked the door behind him, still smiling. Somehow Bryan had made everything right between them again; and undoubtedly his advice was sound. She should see Niall and hear what he had to say. Once the mystery of his reappearance was explained he would assume his proper place in her life; a man whom she had cared for out of all proportion, and mourned sincerely, but not a man who had a place in her present or her future.

CHAPTER SEVEN

JOSS'S sensible attitude towards Niall lasted until about nine o'clock the next morning. She had woken early, bathed and dressed, and then carefully studied the plans for the clinic, wanting to have as many facts as possible at her fingertips before meeting the contractor. Her partners would be there as well, Susan and Michael Devon, a husband and wife team who had been in practice for five years and who were as enthusiastic as she about the new venture. The intricacies of plumbing, wiring and partitions occupied Joss's attention until the brass clock on the bookshelves struck nine. The clock was the wedding gift of Bryan's boss, whose position Bryan eventually hoped to fill, and was, Joss was sure, horrendously expensive.

Nine strokes, each mellifluous and perfectly in pitch. Niall should phone in half an hour, she thought. If he was as little as one minute late she would immediately suspect that he had vanished again. He wouldn't be late. Of course he wouldn't.

Why should it matter, Joss? said a little voice in her ear. You don't get upset when Bryan's calls are late. Why should you for Niall's? Bryan is your fiancé, after all. Not Niall.

She had to tell Niall about Bryan today. It was entirely possible that Niall also was engaged, she thought, frowning, for Trilby Henderson-Smythe had not been exactly thrilled to meet Joss. She discovered that she disliked that thought about as much as the prospect of Niall not phoning, got up from the table where she had all the blueprints spread out and began pacing up and down the living-room. She would be moving out of this apartment soon after the wedding, because she and Bryan had signed for a condominium with a view of Lake Ontario. She did not want to think about condominiums. She did not want to think about the wedding. She wanted Niall to phone.

At twenty past nine the telephone rang. Joss ran for it, seized the receiver and gasped, 'Hello?'

'Hello, Joss. Are you free after your ten o'clock appointment?'

She would have known that voice in the middle of the Sahara. Or in the middle of Toronto. 'I'll be finished about two,' she said; she and her partners were having lunch together.

'I'll have the car—where can I meet you?'

'You're assuming that I want to meet you.'

'That's right.'

Although his confidence irked her, it was fully justified. 'I'll be at the corner of Queen and University at two-fifteen,' she said crisply.

'Wear a red rose.'

The receiver went dead. Joss put it down slowly and remembered walking along a sun-dappled dirt road beside a river. She had been happy then. She was happy now. Happy in a way she had not been for years.

Nursing that happiness, for it was too new to take for granted, she went into her bedroom to get dressed. She had planned to wear a severely cut navy blue dress, having the vague idea that contractors preferred to deal with men; instead she put on a red knit skirt, a long white top and a loose jacket splashed with huge red flowers that might or might not be roses. She was smiling irrepressibly when she left the apartment. The contractor, who reminded her strongly of her brother Harvey, was as anxious as she to get the work done quickly, and she and her partners talked non-stop throughout lunch. They dropped Joss near City Hall at

ten past two, and she walked past the fountain and
Nathan Phillips Square to the corner of Queen and
University.

The sun was shining. A breeze blew her gored skirt
about her legs and teased her hair, and she was
somehow not surprised to hear a piercing wolf whistle
emanate from a dark green sports car illegally parked by
the corner. A dark-haired man was waving at her from
the driver's seat. The tingling sense of anticipation that
Joss had carried with her all morning burst into
happiness again. She gave the man a wide, incautious
smile and ran across the pavement towards him. 'You
called, sir?' she said primly.

In a Humphrey Bogart drawl Niall said, 'Get in the
car, baby. You wanna good time, I'll show it to you.'

She got in. 'Where's your fedora?'

'You dames are all alike . . . complain, complain.' He
grinned at her. 'Hello, beautiful. How are you?'

He looked wonderful: young, vital, blazingly full of
life, very different from the gaunt man with the haunted
eyes whom she had known so long ago. She said
inadequately, 'I'm fine. There's a policeman watching
you from across the street.'

'He's just envious.' Niall pulled out into the traffic.
'We'll go somewhere by the water so we can talk . . .
you're not trying to pass those flowers off as roses,
Joss?'

She glanced down at her jacket. 'They're red.'

'A new hybrid, perhaps. You'll find the real article in
the back seat—a present for you.'

A tissue-wrapped bundle was lying on the seat. Joss
reached for it and began to unwrap it. It contained a
huge spray of glorious red flowers that were indubitably
roses. She buried her nose in them. 'They even smell like
roses,' she marvelled. 'You didn't buy these in a shop,
Niall.'

'I grew them. In a greenhouse.'

'They're beautiful, thank you.' She looked at him sideways. 'So you're not a harried executive any more, Niall? You take time to smell the roses?'

'I'm a harried market gardener instead. For the past four years I've owned three hundred acres north of Toronto in the Humber Valley. I'm into organic gardening—none of these damned chemicals that we're poisoning the earth with.'

Joss said faintly, 'For the past six years I've been at the University of Western Ontario—scarcely a hundred miles from you.'

'I looked for you,' he said violently. 'I remembered that you'd talked about medical school, so I got in touch with Western and Dalhousie, and when that failed, with every research lab in the Halifax area. Same answer at all of them. Sorry, sir, no one here by the name of Jocelyn Gayle.'

Joss looked at him, appalled. 'Jocelyn Gayle isn't my real name—it was the name I used at the Red Lion,' she said. 'I *must* have told you my real name.'

He braked sharply at a set of lights. 'You're kidding,' he said flatly.

'My real name is MacDougall. But Mr Jodrey at the Red Lion didn't like the sound of Joss MacDougall— not romantic enough. So I became Jocelyn Gayle.'

'No wonder I couldn't find you,' Niall said savagely. 'I even went to your apartment building. Sorry, sir, no forwarding address.'

'Magda got married that autumn. So we went our separate ways.'

'And all this time you've been less than a two-hour drive away from me . . . how the gods must have laughed.'

The traffic surged ahead. Niall changed lanes to get on the expressway heading west. Joss sat quietly; her instinct six years ago to remain in Ontario on the chance of meeting Niall again had been perfectly valid. 'What made you choose the Humber Valley?' she asked.

'I wanted to be as close to Toronto as possible . . . I thought by some miracle we might meet again. Why did you choose Western?'

'Same reason.'

'I even went through all the Nova Scotia phone books looking for the name Gayle—you'd never told me the name of your home town. Luckily it's a sparsely populated province.'

'When did you do all this?' she said in a low voice.

'About a year after we met.'

Although Joss knew there were many more questions to ask, she was crushed by the terrible waste of all the months and years that she and Niall had been apart. She said at random, 'I always wondered why I didn't have some sort of intuitive sense of your death. I was sure I would know . . . because of my gypsy grandmother, if nothing else. I understand now, of course, why I didn't.'

Niall was staring straight ahead of him. 'It went deep with you, Joss.'

There was no point in denial. 'Yes. With you as well, I presume. There must be quite a lot of phone books in Nova Scotia.'

His laugh was devoid of humour. 'Deep enough that I suppose subconsciously I've been looking for you ever since.' The traffic light at the intersection ahead of them turned amber, so he braked to a halt. 'This is a long light; I should have taken it,' he muttered.

I've been looking for you ever since . . . 'There's no hurry,' Joss answered absently.

He turned in his seat. 'I still can't believe you're sitting beside me, Joss,' he said. Almost tentatively, as though he was afraid she would disappear if he touched her, he reached out his hand and lifted one of hers from her lap, bringing it to his lips. Her fingers were warm; fleetingly he closed his eyes.

For Joss, the six years fell away as if they had never been: the man she had always been waiting for was here beside her. Her eyes filled with tears.

Niall looked up. With an inarticulate groan he seized her in his arms and kissed her, his mouth ravishing hers, his hands moulding her shoulders, finding the softness of her breast under the loose flowered jacket, straining her as close to his body as he could in the confines of the car.

Behind them a horn blared. Niall said an unprintable word, thrust Joss away from him and drove across the intersection. 'I suppose I should apologise for that,' he said roughly. 'But I'm not going to.'

Joss straightened her clothes with trembling fingers and said nothing. Her mind was blank, her body on fire. Clutching the edges of her jacket, she remembered the sureness of his hand on her breast and her own leaping, instinctive response, and was afraid.

Niall glanced over his shoulder before changing lanes; Joss's head was downbent. 'Say something, Joss, for God's sake,' he pleaded.

She made a small, helpless movement with her hands. 'I don't know what to say.'

'I shouldn't have kissed you like that,' he said violently. 'Maybe I had to prove that you were real . . . words can be so damned inadequate.'

'Yes,' she said faintly; she could not have agreed more.

To her relief he put on his signal light. 'We'll turn off here, there's a park down by the water.'

People were flying kites in the park, the bright squares of silk like a colourful parade in the sky. Joss got out of the car, thrusting her hands in her pockets of her jacket as she and Niall began to stroll across the grass. 'Why did you start looking for me a year after we met?' she said in a carefully emotionless voice.

He accepted her lead. 'To explain that, I'd better

begin at the beginning . . . I was given the original
diagnosis in Vancouver, which is where I was living at
the time. But I have a very good friend in the medical
profession in Toronto, so I came east to get a second
opinion. The day I talked to Magda was the day the
prognosis was confirmed—less than a year. The next
day, by one of those crazy strokes of fate, I met you. I
knew the moment I laid eyes on you that you and I were
meant for each other. What I should have done was
walk out of the Red Lion and never go back. But I
couldn't—the pull was too strong. So then I figured that
if we spent some time together I'd find out that you
were just an ordinary woman, no one to get excited
about, and that love at first sight was a myth
perpetuated by the pulp magazines. I found out
differently, of course—I don't have to tell you that.' He
stopped on the path, the wind ruffling his hair, his eyes
like fragments of the sky. 'So I ran away, Joss. I didn't
know what else to do.'

'You could have stayed,' she answered, all the
bitterness of those wasted years in her voice. 'We could
have gone through it together.'

As if he were explaining himself to a child, Niall said
patiently, 'Joss, I thought I was going to *die*.'

'We all have to one day. Why couldn't I have been
with you?'

'I couldn't do that to you,' he said implacably.

'Relationships aren't just built on good times,
Niall—you share bad times as well,' she answered just
as implacably.

'Look, I'd read every book I could lay my hands on
about the type of cancer I had, so I knew what it could
do to me—do you think I could expose you to that?
What kind of person would that have made me?'

'A person capable of being real,' Joss said emphati-
cally.

'A totally selfish person,' Niall retorted. He began

walking towards the water again. 'So I flew back to Vancouver that Sunday morning, and a month later my friend in Toronto called. A brand-new drug was being tested in the States. He knew the director of the clinic in Boston, and if I wanted to go I could be a guinea pig. So I went—what did I have to lose? For six months I went through hell, because some of the side-effects were horrific. But at the end of a year the tumour had disappeared—which is when I started looking for you.'

'If only I'd told you my right name!'

Niall turned to face her again. 'Maybe it's better that we didn't meet then. You see, they said down in Boston that if in five years there was no recurrence then I was completely cured. The five years are up in three weeks, Joss. I feel great, and I'm ninety-nine per cent sure they'll give me a clean bill of health at my check-up. Which means that in three weeks you and I could start all over again.'

He was smiling at her, and she saw in his eyes a vast upwelling of tenderness. Her face felt stiff and there was a sinking sensation in the pit of her stomach. She said tonelessly, 'I'm getting married two weeks from Saturday.'

Behind them the kites snapped in the wind. Joss's skirt flapped against her legs. The smile had faded from Niall's face. 'You're serious, aren't you?' he said finally.

'Yes. St David's Church in North York at two o'clock in the afternoon. The invitations have all been sent.'

'But you're not wearing an engagement ring.'

'I didn't want one.'

'Are you marrying the man in the restaurant?'

'Yes. I met him two years ago. You see, I stopped looking for you five years ago, Niall.'

He flinched. 'Yes—of course you would have . . . I'm not blaming you, Joss. But, my God, I thought we'd been given a second chance!'

Her hands were clenched in her pockets. 'I guess life doesn't work that way.'

For a few moments Niall stood still, staring at the ground, his face concentrated in thought. Then he said, 'You were in love with me six years ago, weren't you, Joss?'

As well to deny that the sun rose in the east. 'Yes, I was.'

'Do you feel the same way about this man?'

'His name is Bryan,' she said irritably. 'You know that. He's a doctor. And he's a very different person from you; how could I feel the same way?'

'Remember the riverbank? Did you go to bed with him the first time you were alone together?'

She paled. 'I was young and naïve then, Niall. I'm older now.'

He gripped her elbow; lines were etched in his face. 'We never went to bed, did we, Joss? But we'd have been good together, you know that as well as I do. Is he as good? Is he, Joss?'

She shook her arm free, her eyes glittering. 'That's none of your business!'

'So he's not.'

'I never said that! How dare you think you can reappear in my life and pick up where you left off and ask me all kinds of impertinent questions?' she cried incoherently. '*You're* the one who disappeared, Niall Morgan, remember that!'

'I take full responsibility for that,' he said heavily. 'And if you were engaged to someone who made you ecstatically happy, even though it would break my heart, I'd step back and be happy for you. But you don't look ecstatically happy. And I remember your honesty, Joss—if you and this guy were fantastic in bed, you'd tell me so.'

'I've never been to bed with him!'

There was a perceptible silence. 'Has he got iced

water in his veins?'

'He's old-fashioned enough to want to wait until we're married.'

Niall said silkily, 'You and I wouldn't have waited. And look how you responded to me in the car, Joss.'

She wanted to cover her ears and scream that he was crazy. 'Niall, you've got to stop this! I love Bryan and I'm going to marry him.'

'If it kills you,' Niall said grimly.

'I'm doing the right thing,' she retorted.

'Don't you see what a cruel joke this is? That you're getting married just a few days before I have my final check-up?'

It was Joss's turn to pause. Then she said with ominous quietness, 'Are you telling me that if Bryan didn't exist, you and I would not be getting involved again until *after* your check-up?'

'If we've waited six years, what's another three weeks?'

She said evenly, 'So you're still looking for guarantees.'

'I have to know that I'm cured!'

'People who love each other and live together don't vanish if one or the other of them gets ill. They hang in—that's what love's all about.'

'But we're not living together. I can't take that kind of risk, not when a mere three weeks would remove it.'

Joss said hopelessly, 'You haven't learned a damned thing from the past six years, Niall Morgan. You're still running.'

'Maybe you're doing the same,' Niall said in an ugly voice. 'Why else are you marrying an uptight professional who hasn't got the guts to take you to bed?'

'Let me tell you something,' she flared. 'I've never gone to bed with anyone! I told you why six years ago—because I hadn't met the right man. *You* were the

right man. I knew that. Four hours, four days, four
years, it wouldn't have made the slightest
difference—you were *right*. But you took off, didn't
you? You vanished. Once Magda told me what the
problem was I turned Toronto upside-down trying to
find you. But I couldn't find you. I couldn't find you
anywhere. So I mourned you instead, and for the best
part of three years I didn't even go out on a date. Then I
met Bryan. I respect him, I like him, I'm going to marry
him. *He'll* never disappear. Not like you.'

To her horror, her voice had broken and her eyes had
filled with tears. She turned her back on Niall, trying to
focus on the wavering horizon of the lake.

For several seconds Niall said nothing. Then he
brought her round to face him. Putting his arms around
her, he held her close in a way that was different from
the way he had held her in the car.

He was wearing a sweater over a shirt. Joss could hear
the rhythm of his heart and was encircled by the
strength of his arms and knew she had never forgotten
his embrace; it had been engraved on her, and nothing
Bryan had ever done had erased it. She knew something
else. This time, she was sure, Niall had only intended to
comfort her. But along with a sense of utter security his
closeness was arousing other feelings, feelings that until
today had been buried for years. She wanted him just as
fiercely now as she had at the river's edge, she thought
with painful truth; just as fiercely as she had in the car.
As she raised a face to him that was full of doubt and
confusion, he bent his head and kissed her.

The sweetness of honey, the unfolding of apple blossoms, all the promise of spring was in his kiss. Joss
clung to him, abandoning herself to the warmth of his
lips and her own hunger, that eclipsed reason and
restraint. She felt alive again, fully alive, a desirable
woman whose body had been fashioned with needs that
only Niall could meet.

Against her lips Niall muttered, 'We must observe some kind of decorum—this is a public park. Joss, you can't marry this guy. You still love me.'

She felt as if she had been dunked in the cold waters of Lake Ontario. She pulled back and said, not very sensibly, 'What have I *done*?'

'It's not what you've done, it's what we've done,' Niall said with aggravating logic. 'We've discovered that the old magic is still there. We're dynamite together, Joss. We were six years ago and we still are. So you can't marry your precious doctor.'

She threw caution to the winds as if it were a kite. 'So go to the city hall,' she said trenchantly, 'and get a special licence. You and I could get married this weekend.'

His face hardened. 'You're playing games.'

'You mean the answer's no?'

'In three weeks I'll be in the clear, Joss!'

'In three weeks I'll be married to Bryan.'

'You'll be making a hell of a mistake.'

'As big a mistake as you made six years ago when you got on the plane to Vancouver?'

'I'll never see that as a mistake!'

'How can we possibly get married when we have such radically different views about the nature of love?' Joss said despairingly. 'Love isn't just dynamite sex, Niall. It's being together . . . for better, for worse, in sickness and in health.'

'Then we're at an impasse,' he said levelly.

A turquoise kite with a long pink tail suddenly lost its balance and did a spectacular nosedive. At the last moment the handler saved it from collision with the ground. It lurched upwards, then soared freely on the wind again. Joss had watched all this. She said thoughtfully, 'Niall, can you tell me why you feel the way you do? You mentioned once that your mother died many years ago—is it something to do with that?'

With a steel edge to his voice he said, 'Now who's asking impertinent questions?'

She raised her chin. 'I'm only trying to understand.'

He sighed. Then he said with a visible effort at control, 'We've been dealing with some pretty high-powered emotions here, Joss. Why don't we cool it for a while? Let's walk down to those birches by the water and you can tell me about medical school and I'll tell you about market gardening.'

So she was not to be given the reason. She managed a small smile. 'Sounds like a good idea to me.'

Milky waves were slopping against the stone abutment and a few lazy seagulls hovered over the picnic area as Joss and Niall began to talk. Two hours later they were still talking, with the ease and camaraderie of two people who are in tune. Joss had been describing the clinic to Niall, drawing a rough plan of the layout on her notepad, when she caught sight of her watch. 'Is that the time?' she squeaked.

He checked his own watch, the same one he had six years ago. 'You're two minutes slow.'

'I've got to go! I'm meeting Bryan for dinner at his mother's tonight.'

'So we're back to reality,' Niall said drily.

Joss still couldn't believe the time could have passed so quickly. 'Yes, I guess we are.'

'What are we going to do, Joss? Will we see each other again?'

'I don't know,' she said helplessly. 'I simply don't know.'

'I want to.' He took the notepad from her lax fingers. 'I'll give you my phone number—business and home. You can call me any time, Joss.'

With a flash of spirit she said, 'I won't interrupt you with Ms Trilby Henderson-Smythe?'

'You will not. A casual date, Joss. The only kind I've had the last five years.'

She got up from the bench, shoving the notepad back in her purse, knowing whatever happened she would cherish the piece of paper with Niall's handwriting on it. Avoiding his eyes she said, 'I really have to go, Niall. Could you drop me off near a subway stop?'

'I'll take you to your apartment.'

'I'd rather you didn't. Bryan might get there early to pick me up.'

'I see,' he said quietly. 'This is a difficult situation, isn't it?'

Understatement of the year, she thought unhappily. 'Look at that kite, it's got five separate sections,' she said.

They talked about kites, the poor conditions of the expressway and a recent warehouse fire until Niall pulled up by a subway station. Then he said abruptly, 'So is this it, Joss? You'll get married in two weeks and we'll never see each other again?'

'I can't deceive Bryan!' she cried. 'I won't go behind his back.'

'You always were honest, Joss.'

'If I'm honest, I feel as though I'm being torn apart,' she said in a ragged voice.

'Then tell him you're still in love with me.'

'I thought I loved him!'

Niall banged the flat of his hand against the steering wheel. 'I'll call you in the next couple of days. You'd better go, you'll be late.'

His profile was turned to her, his jaw set. She said breathlessly, 'Goodbye,' and scrambled out of the car. Not until she was on the subway platform did she realise that she had left the red roses in the back seat of the car.

CHAPTER EIGHT

To JOSS'S great relief, Bryan was not waiting for her at the apartment. She changed into tailored beige trousers with a crocheted sweater and tried consciously to relax, for her brain was whirling and her eyes overbright. When Bryan arrived she found herself turning her cheek to his kiss and hustling him out of the apartment right away. When they were headed north on Yonge Street Bryan said, 'I tried to call you this afternoon.'

'I met Niall after lunch.'

'That was probably a wise move, Joss. Get it out of your system.'

She remembered the kiss by the lake and winced inwardly at her duplicity. 'I suppose so.'

'You won't be seeing him again.'

Bryan had made it a statement, not a question. She felt a flicker of rebellion, squashed it, and said, 'I'll be busy with the clinic and with the wedding.'

'Mother says more gifts have arrived.'

Bryan's mother Leah, of whom Joss was very fond, was happily doing the lion's share of the wedding preparations. She was an attractive widow who had a sparkle that her son lacked. She greeted Joss with a kiss. 'Lovely to see you, dear. Bryan darling, pour some drinks, will you? Three huge boxes arrived today, Joss. I'm dying for you to open them.'

Wedding presents, thought Joss numbly. She had to unwrap them, write thank-you letters, store them in her apartment, then move them to the condominium after the wedding. After the wedding . . . *Niall*.

'Joss, are you all right?' Leah said sharply.

126

Joss gave her head a little shake. 'Must be pre-nuptial nerves,' she joked, heard the tension in her voice and knew Leah must have heard it, too.

The first box contained a very lovely hand-turned wooden salad set, the second a marble lamp whose base reminded Joss of a headstone, and the third a ceramic ornament, four feet tall, replete with fat bunches of grapes and smirking cupids. Joss looked at it in horror, for it seemed to express the debasement of passion to a simpering, mass-produced sweetness. I can't give Bryan passion, she thought frantically. I'll never be able to.

'Well,' said Leah, 'you could always hide it at the very back of the garden.'

'We won't have a garden,' Joss said. She, who had grown up on a farm, was going to be living on the tenth floor of a high-rise. She couldn't grow roses if she wanted to. She closed her eyes, feeling the wings of panic beat about her head.

Bryan put his hand on her shoulder. She jumped, splashing some of her drink on her trousers, fighting a ridiculous urge to burst into tears.

'I'll get a cloth,' Leah said briskly.

'I'm beginning to wonder what happened this afternoon,' Bryan said stiffly, his grey eyes very watchful.

'Nothing!'

'You're not yourself at all.'

'Of course I am—I'm fine. It's just . . . oh thank you, Leah.' Joss made a valiant effort to pull herself together, and the rest of the evening went more smoothly. After she and Bryan had lugged the boxes up to her apartment, she closed the spare room door on them and said with perfect truth, 'I'm really tired, Bryan. I think I'll go to bed.'

He put his arms around her. She stared at his immaculate shirt-front and old school tie and heard him say, 'Joss, you're not going to back out of the wedding, are you?'

The tie had a pattern of tiny gold unicorns. 'Seeing Niall today upset me,' she blurted.

'The invitations are out, the presents are arriving, all my colleagues are invited—it would be extremely awkward to call the whole thing off.'

'A wedding should be more than a social occasion,' she protested.

'I wish to God I'd taken you to any restaurant other than Scarlatti's last night!'

Bryan almost never swore. 'Better to have met Niall now than two weeks after the wedding.'

'Better never to have met him at all. He's part of your past, Joss.'

She had the beginnings of a headache. 'I thought he was,' she whispered.

'He is. You and I belong together. We have all kinds of interests in common, and you know how fond of you my mother is.'

But were those sufficient reasons to get married? Joss wondered, and felt again the flutterings of panic. Then Bryan raised her chin and kissed her and panic exploded into denial. She shoved him away. 'Please don't!' she gasped.

'Joss, I'm your fiancé!'

'I don't know what's wrong with me. I feel like I'm being torn apart.' She had used the same words with Niall, she remembered with a touch of desperation.

In a cold voice Bryan said, 'I don't want you to see that man again, Joss. Ever. He's bad for you. Everything was fine until he came along.'

Never to see Niall again? Impossible. 'You can't turn the clock back,' she said.

'You can avoid making the same mistake twice. He abandoned you six years ago; he could do the same thing again.'

In three weeks he could do the same thing again, she

thought wildly. The headache had become a pounding reality. 'Bryan, I'll do the best I can and I promise I won't deceive you. That's all I can say—except goodnight,' she added with a fractional smile.

'It's little enough,' he said huffily. 'Goodnight, Joss.'

She went to bed as soon as he had gone, and dreamed of ceramic grapes tossed with red rose petals in a wooden salad bowl.

Joss spent the morning at her apartment tidying up some correspondence and reading medical journals. The phone rang once during the entire morning, and it was neither Niall nor Bryan. It was Magda.

Magda's faith in Charlie had been fully justified. He had patented two inexpensive pollution control devices for the pulp and paper industry four years ago, and he and Magda now lived in an architecturally designed house on Crescent Road. They were expecting their first child any day and had become, to Joss's amusement, mini-encyclopaedias of obstetrical lore.

'Hi, Joss. Not a labour pain in sight,' Magda groaned.

Joss, the medical expert, said soothingly, 'You can't rush nature, Magda.'

Magda discussed various internal details at some length, then said more cheerfully, 'And how are you?'

'In a mess,' Joss replied succinctly, and proceeded to describe the events of the last two days. It was a great relief to talk about Niall to someone who knew the whole story.

Magda listened in a fascinated silence, then said, 'It's very simple. Tell Bryan the wedding's off and marry Niall.'

'Before or after the check-up?' Joss snorted.

'He can't disappear a second time, Joss, not if he's got a three-hundred-acre farm just outside the city.'

'He hasn't asked me to marry him.'

'Well, you are engaged to someone else.'

'Bryan is afraid I'm going to change my mind.'

'Bryan's not a bad guy,' Magda said judiciously. 'He loves his job, he's nice to his mother, he's an upright citizen who'll never get a speeding ticket in his life. But you don't light up when he comes in the room, Joss. After six years, when Charlie comes home after work I still feel as though someone's turned on every light bulb in the house.'

'You're no help,' Joss said crossly.

'You've been given a second chance—take it, that's all.'

'Easy for you to say—you don't have a spare room full of wedding presents.' Joss proceeded to describe the ceramic cherubs.

After Magda had rung off Joss went out to do some errands. Then, on impulse, she headed down to the clinic. The workmen were tearing down partitions and ripping out the old plumbing fixtures; dust motes fogged the air. Joss stepped over a pile of old lumber and went into the room that would eventually be her office. The grimy-paned window looked out on the peeling paint of the next-door tenement. She ran her finger along the sill. She'd put plants on it, she thought, and hang her credentials on the wall beside it. Here in this room she had no doubts as to who she was . . .

Behind her a familiar male voice said, 'Dr MacDougall?'

Somehow not at all surprised to hear that voice, Joss adopted a businesslike smile and turned around. 'Good afternoon, Mr Morgan.'

'I know I haven't got an appointment,' Niall said. 'But I'm suffering from the most disturbing symptoms.'

'Would you describe them for me, please?'

He said promptly, 'Palpitations of the heart, weakness in the knees, sweating palms . . . plus one other effect I'd be embarrassed to describe to you. But I only get these symptoms when I'm with a twenty-seven-year-old blonde who had gold flecks in her eyes.'

'You could stop seeing the blonde,' Joss suggested.

He put his head to one side. 'Lurid dreams,' he added. 'I forgot to mention those. The kind you wouldn't tell your mother . . . doctors are not supposed to blush.'

'*You're* not supposed to be here.' Nor was she supposed to feel so incredibly happy to see him—a symptom she kept to herself.

'I wanted to see your clinic. Will this be your office?'

A plank rasped free across the hall, followed by the thud of falling plaster. 'If you have faith in miracles,' said Joss, and began to describe the layout. She was soon carried away by her enthusiasm and by Niall's evident interest; his questions were intelligent, and one or two of his suggestions well worth investigating. They ended their tour at the front door, where two chipped porcelain basins lay drunkenly on the pavement.

Niall looked up and down the street, which looked depressingly tawdry. 'You might want to hire a male receptionist,' he remarked. 'Someone who's been a bouncer in a nightclub, for instance.'

'Not a bad idea,' she said drily.

'Is your fiancé involved in this?'

'No. He'd like to see me practising paediatrics in one of the snootier suburbs.'

Niall made a noise loosely translated as, 'Humph.' Then he said, 'This street is about as far from the farm as you can get, Joss.'

'I like Toronto a lot better than I used to,' she answered defensively. 'And of course Bryan works in the city. But I don't know that I'll ever feel at home here.'

'You can take the girl out of the country, but not the reverse.'

She did not want to talk about the farm or the

country. 'Niall, why are you here?'

He moved to one side to allow a workman to dump a load of old lathes on the pavement. 'I had to see you. When I called your apartment there was no answer, so I figured you might be down here.'

'I thought we'd agreed we wouldn't see each other again.'

'We didn't agree on anything.'

'I'm engaged to Bryan!'

'The symptoms are real, Joss.'

She said levelly. 'Take me with you when you go to Boston for your check-up.'

'No. But I'll call you as soon as I get back.'

'If the results are positive,' she retorted bitterly.

His gaze was unflinching. 'That's right,' he said.

'Niall, go away,' she said with the calmness of despair. 'This is lunacy. I can't bear to be hurt by you all over again, I just can't bear it. I love Bryan and I'm going to marry him. Go away and leave me alone!'

Another workman had lugged two buckets of broken plaster out of the building. ''Scuse me, miss,' he said.

Hurriedly Joss stepped aside. It was beginning to rain, and in a burst of ill-temper she cried, 'Of all the hundreds of restaurants in Toronto, why did Bryan have to pick Scarlatti's?'

'We'd have met sooner or later. Joss, don't marry him.'

'You've got a nerve!' she exploded. 'You want me to break my engagement and change my whole life, even though you're not prepared to change a damn thing. No, sir—you're going to play it safe and wait until you've got a nice little certificate of health in your hand before *you* make any commitments.'

'If you marry him we'll never have a chance.'

'I'll marry whom I please,' Joss said furiously.

Niall was white about the mouth. 'I'm begging you not to marry Bryan.'

Suddenly she could not bear the turmoil of emotion in her breast. 'I've had enough of this—go away, Niall,' she said breathlessly. 'I'm going inside to get my coat, and when I come back I want you to be gone.'

He said with icy precision, 'If I go I won't be back.'

She ignored a hot stab of pain that seemed to pierce her to the core. 'Good!' she snapped, pivoted and ran back in the building. Stumbling over the uneven boards, she went into her office. She did not have a coat there; she had known she would not have the courage to stand on the pavement and watch Niall drive away.

A wrecking bar clanged to the floor in the next room, and the steady whump of a mallet seemed to echo her heartbeat. Joss stared out of the window, counting slowly to one hundred. Then she went back outside. Niall's sports car was gone.

It was raining harder, spotting her beige trousers, dampening her hair, bouncing on the roof of her car. Niall had taken her at her word. He had gone. And she knew him well enough to be sure he would not be back.

She crossed the road very slowly, her heart still beating with the heavy strokes of the workman's mallet. A disagreeable symptom, Dr MacDougall, she thought wretchedly, and recalled her blind, unreasoning happiness when she had seen Niall standing in the doorway of her office.

He would never stand there again.

She drove home with exaggerated caution. When she opened the door of her apartment the telephone was ringing. She ran across the room and grabbed the receiver. But it was Leah on the line, not Niall. Trying to swallow a disappointment caustic as lye, Joss heard Leah say, 'I'm just down the road, dear. As you're home, can I drop off a brochure from the florists?'

'Sure. I'll put the kettle on,' Joss mumbled, and hung up, trembling in reaction. She had been a fool to think Niall would call. She had told him to stay away, hadn't she?

She was still standing by the phone when the doorbell rang. Leah's hair was freshly tinted and her raincoat the newest fashion. She kissed Joss and remarked, 'You must have got caught in the rain without a coat.'

'Yes,' Joss said vaguely. 'I guess I did.'

Leah put her head to one side. 'Joss, what's wrong? You weren't yourself last night, and Bryan nearly bit my head off when I phoned him at work today.'

Joss met Leah's gaze; Leah's eyes were the same grey as her son's, yet lit by a warmth Bryan showed only rarely. 'I forgot to put the kettle on,' she said.

'Go and change your clothes and dry your hair. I'll make the tea, and then we'll sit down and have a good talk.'

'Is this your bossy mother-in-law act?' Joss asked with something like a genuine smile.

'Someone's got to get bossy around here. Off you go.'

It was comforting to be told what to do; Joss missed her own mother rather more than she would admit. Within five minutes she had changed into a comfortable track suit and was curled up on the chesterfield with a cup of Earl Grey. Then, beginning with her first sight of Niall at the Red Lion six years ago, she told Leah the whole story. She was well into her second cup by the time she finished with the scene on the pavement at Queen Street.

Leah poured herself another cup of tea. 'What you've told me explains so much,' she said reflectively. 'Don't get me wrong, I dearly love my son. But he can be a bit of a stick-in-the-mud—rather like his father—and it's often puzzled me why you chose him. You're so full of warmth and spontaneity, Joss. And—let's use the word—passion. You'd be good for Bryan, I'm sure. But I'm not sure how good he'd be for you.'

'He has been good for me, Leah,' Joss argued. 'He

was really the first man I dated after Niall, and he's been so patient and understanding. I owe him a lot.'

'But do you owe him marriage?'

'I would hardly have expected you of all people to ask that question,' Joss countered in exasperation.

'I care for both of you. Too much to see you make a mistake.'

Leah's smile was singularly sweet. Joss said in a rush, 'I care about you, too. I want to do what's right, Leah. That's what I was trying to do this afternoon by sending Niall away.'

'Right for whom? For Bryan? For Niall? Or for you?'

'For everyone,' Joss said helplessly.

'If Bryan weren't a doctor, would you be as fond of him?'

'I'm not interested in the money he makes!'

'I wasn't suggesting that. But Bryan does excellent work, and because you threw yourself so wholeheartedly into medicine, I wonder if you've ever quite separated him from his job.' Stirring her tea Leah added delicately, 'One doesn't go to bed with a doctor. One goes to bed with a man.'

'I've never gone to bed with Bryan. Or with Niall,' Joss said clumsily.

'So which one would you choose?'

Joss's hesitation went on too long. Leah said gently, 'I see. Be awfully careful, Joss. When sex goes well, it takes its rightful place in marriage. But when it doesn't, it can be horrendous.'

Intuitively Joss knew Leah was speaking of her own marriage, to a man who had been very much like Bryan. 'But if there's any doubt about Niall's condition he'll push me away again.'

'There are two separate problems here, Joss. The first is whether you should marry Bryan—do you honestly believe your feelings for him are strong enough for a lifelong relationship? The second is Niall's inability to share the bad times along with the good. I'm not sure how one would cope with that. But they are two different issues. You're in danger of treating them as one.'

Was Leah right? Joss gave a heavy sigh. 'If I have any more tea I'll be water-logged,' she said. 'I know you're not going to tell me what to do, are you, Leah?'

'Definitely not,' Leah said crisply. 'Although I will say it's easier to break an engagement than to get a divorce.'

'You sound like my friend Magda.'

'You're getting advice from all sides, aren't you, dear? You'll do the right thing, I know.'

Joss wished she could be as sure.

The telephone rang once more that day, about four-thirty. 'Joss, it's Bryan. An emergency's come up at the hospital. A bad fire in Scarborough, a number of children involved, so it looks like it'll be an all-nighter. Can you get someone else to go to the theatre with you?'

She had forgotten that she and Bryan had tickets for *Cats* that evening. 'I'll see if Magda will go with me—it'll take her mind off motherhood. I hope everything will go all right, Bryan.'

'They're calling in extra staff. I'll probably sleep tomorrow morning, but maybe in the afternoon we could go out to the country and find somewhere to eat.'

Joss recognised this as a sacrifice on his part, for Bryan did not like the country. Then he added, 'I go away on Sunday afternoon. You'll take me to the airport, won't you, Joss?'

She had forgotten that, as well. Bryan was going to Switzerland for an international convention and would be away for a week. In a great flood of relief she thought of having a whole week to herself, with time to think and sort out all the emotional chaos of the past three days.

'Joss, are you still there?'

'Of course I'll take you to the airport. Good luck tonight, Bryan, I'll be thinking about you. And I'll see you tomorrow.'

'Thanks. 'Bye.'

His mind, she knew, was more on his upcoming patients than on herself, which did not bother her at all. Quickly she dialled Magda's number.

'Love to,' said Magda. 'I'm sick to death of being pregnant . . . who are you engaged to today?'

'Bryan, of course,' Joss answered haughtily.

'Your conscience is as scrupulous as an archbishop's,' Magda complained.

'I have to try and do what's right.'

'And how does Niall react to that?'

'Niall and I are not on speaking terms,' Joss replied even more haughtily. 'I'm not inviting you out tonight so we can talk about Niall, Magda.'

'Just remember there's a lot more to marriage than the wedding,' Magda said portentously.

'Oh, hush!' Joss said.

Cats, however, successfully distracted Magda from engagements and babies and Joss from weddings. Joss drove Magda home afterwards and slept soundly that night. The next day Bryan was not free until dinner time. He had had less than four hours' sleep since the day before and had to go back to the hospital that evening. He described a number of the cases to Joss, which she knew from experience was his way of rechecking that he had done everything he could. She listened intently, putting in the occasional question, realising what a bond this sort of conversation was. He looked very tired. She kissed him goodnight with genuine affection, almost glad she was not on speaking terms with Niall, for she could be fairer to Bryan this way. The next afternoon she drove Bryan to the airport.

'Don't come in,' he said as he unlocked the trunk and

took out his suitcase. 'I'm going to the first-class lounge to snatch a half-hour's sleep.'

'You've put in some long hours since Friday.'

'Mother regularly accuses me of being a workaholic.' He smiled at Joss. 'I've felt better about our relationship the last couple of days, though. I think we're over the hump.' Then he kissed her goodbye very thoroughly and disappeared through the sliding doors.

As Joss watched his upright figure vanish into the crowd the tight coil of tension that had been with her since the evening at Scarlatti's began to loosen. A week to herself. A week to relax. A week to decide.

This plan, however, lasted for only the first hour she was home. Then Michael Devon, one of her two prospective clinic partners, phoned her. His wife Susan was ill. Could Joss take over her practice for the week?

Joss sputtered a number of ifs and buts, agreed to do so, spent Sunday evening with Michael familiarising herself with the set-up, and then worked all week as hard as she had ever worked in her internship. The work was exhilarating and exhausting and she loved it; on Friday it was past midnight when she got to bed.

Nevertheless, Joss woke early on Saturday morning. Her first thought was that a week from today she was supposed to be marrying Bryan; her second was to wonder what Niall was doing; her third that she was to meet Bryan at the airport the following afternoon and she did not seem to have made any kind of decision. She buried her face in the pillow, cravenly trying to obliterate all thought. But she could not go back to sleep. She got up and prowled around the apartment, filled with a strange restlessness. The sun was shining. It was a beautiful May morning. What was she doing cooped up in an apartment in the city?

Not stopping to think, she dressed in shorts and a cotton top, grabbed a banana for breakfast and went down in the lift to the car park. Her aged Volkswagen started on the first try, which seemed a good omen to Joss, who then chugged out of the garage and headed north, out of the city. The tenth exit on the turnpike named the little town of Braxton. Niall's farm was on the outskirts of Braxton. She took the exit.

Braxton was ten kilometres to the west. The road meandered between low-lying hills covered with newly leafed birch trees that were loud with birdsong. Joss stopped by a brook and picked a bunch of violets, their little white faces veined with purple among heart-shaped green leaves. She felt suspended in time and space. If she was as intent upon doing the right thing as she kept telling everyone, she should not be anywhere in the vicinity of Niall's home. Yet a strange impulse had brought her here; and although she felt as shy and tentative as the violets poking up between the rocks, she knew she would not turn back.

She packed the violet stems in wet moss, got in her car and drove on. Five minutes later she came to a very attractive scrolled sign beside a narrow lane that disappeared into the trees. Morgan's Market Gardens, said the sign. Fruit Trees. Shrubs. Strawberries.

She turned into the lane, which was overhung with oak and beech trees; long ago Joss had decided that there was no green quite as fresh as a newly unfurled beech leaf. She discovered that she was singing to herself.

The lane climbed steadily up an incline, then widened in front of a small, grey-painted cabin. Two mongrels rushed up to meet her, barking enthusiastically. A cat that reminded her of Magda's Nasturtium—who now presided over the architecturally designed house— yawned at her from a sunlit bench in front of the cabin. The other occupant of the bench was a wizened old man in a pair of incredibly dirty dungarees. Joss got out of the car.

The cabin was flanked by forsythia bushes like min-

iature sunbursts. The air smelled clean and sweet. Joss
smiled at the old man and said, 'Is Niall Morgan here,
please?'

The old man screwed up his face. 'Yeah. He's here.'

'Where would I find him?'

'You want to buy trees, or shrubs?'

'Neither. I just want to see Niall.' Which was the
simple truth, she thought in wonderment.

'You the dame he's mooning over?'

She looked straight into his rheumy old eyes. 'Who
are you?' she responded.

'Name's Clem.' He spat in the dust. 'Known Niall
since he stood no taller than a gooseberry bush.'

'He *told* you about me?'

'Him?' Clem gave a cackle of laughter. 'Not likely.
Never known any one so close-mouthed. But I'm no
fool, I saw him pick them roses. I c'n put two and two
together and get three and a half any day of the week.'

Joss leaned against the side of her car. 'Did you say
you knew him when he was a little boy?'

'Yep.' Clem fondled the ears of the brown and white
mongrel, who was sniffing the cuffs of his disgraceful
dungarees.

'Tell me how his mother died,' Joss demanded.

Clem leered at her. 'Now that's a funny question
from a pretty little thing like you.'

'Don't be sexist. It will help me understand him.'

Clem gave another cackle of laughter. 'He's like one
of them hedgehogs—touch 'em and they curl up in a
ball. He ain't into being understood.'

'Did she have a long illness?' Joss persisted.

'Say, you're sure curious. You know what curiosity
did to the cat?'

'*You're* exasperating!' Joss snapped. 'Why won't you
tell me?'

'Ask him, not me. It was his mother.' Clem tipped the
brim of his cap. 'You gonna marry him?'

Joss said sweetly, 'Ask him, not me.'

'So you got spunk.' Another leer. 'I'll tell you somethin'. Everythin' was kept very hush-hush those years his ma was ill. But he changed . . . yeah, he sure changed.' Abruptly Clem stood up, dislodging the mongrel. 'I got work to do. Drive past the house and you'll hear the tiller, he's workin' up a new bed.' Clem cackled again. 'Not the kind you're interested in,' he said. Then he whistled to the dogs and disappeared behind the cabin. Joss, red-faced, got in her car and drove down the hill.

The house, made of stone, nestled in the valley. Newly planted fields took up the flats, orchards striped the slopes, quince and rhododendrons and azaleas edged the road. Joss drove past the house, which had a blue front door flanked by trumpet honeysuckle, and parked the car. The growl of a roto-tiller came from her left. She walked up the slope.

Niall, stripped to the waist, his hands protected by heavy gloves, was throwing rocks into a wheelbarrow. Then he turned back to the tiller, engaged the gear, and began churning up the rich black earth. Beyond the garden a grove of cherry trees was in bloom.

It was not the orchard back home, thought Joss with a catch at her heart. But it was near enough. She stepped from between two forsythia bushes and waved at the blue-eyed man in the garden.

CHAPTER NINE

NIALL saw Joss immediately. He turned off the tiller and into the ringing silence said quietly, 'Joss . . . am I dreaming?'

'No, I'm real.'

He pulled off his gloves, draped them on the handle of the tiller and walked towards her, his boots sinking into the soil. 'Are you alone? No fiancé?'

'He's away,' she said. Bryan had no place in this beautiful valley.

Niall stopped a couple of feet away from her. 'But he's still your fiancé?'

'Yes.' Niall's chest was slicked with sweat; there was a daub of mud on his shoulder. She fought the urge to wipe it off and wondered dizzily what she was doing here.

As if he had read her thoughts, he asked, 'Why are you here?'

'I . . . don't know.'

The sun was full on her face. 'You look tired,' he said.

'I put in some long hours this week.' Quickly Joss explained about Susan's practice.

Niall said gravely, 'So you thought you'd go for a drive this morning, and when you saw my sign you decided to drop in.'

She smiled, knowing he was as glad to see her as she was to see him, knowing also he was not going to ask any more awkward questions. 'You need a coffee break.'

'You can stay for coffee, for lunch and for dinner. But I'm warning you, I'll probably put you to work.'

The scent of freshly turned earth teased her nostrils. 'There's nothing I'd like better.'

'What do you think of the place, Joss?'

She looked up at him and said softly, 'It's an enchanted place.'

Without laying a finger on her, Niall bent his head. Their lips met in a long, drugged kiss that left Joss weak with desire. She wanted to rest her cheek on his chest and inhale the mingling of sweat and soil on his skin; she wanted to hold the scarred ribs under her palm and keep him safe. He was real to her, real in a way Bryan had never been. How could she marry Bryan? she wondered; and wondered also if the decision was not making itself, if her visit here this morning was not in its own way a decision. Quite unable to share any of this, she said weakly, 'Coffee.'

Niall lifted one brow. 'Iced water?'

She laughed and suddenly everything was all right. As they wandered towards the house, Niall explained how he was developing the property, and his plans for the future. The house had beautifully proportioned rooms that were extremely clean but very bare; all Niall's energies had gone into the outdoors, thought Joss, her imagination stirred by so many blank walls and empty corridors. None of the blank walls in the condominium had stirred her at all.

After they had drunk cold orange juice on the patio, they worked together at the new garden for a couple of hours, Joss happily taking her turn at lugging rocks, her slender calves lost in a pair of Niall's work boots. Then Niall said, wiping his forehead, 'You know what we should do? Let's pack a picnic and take the canoe out on the lake.'

'You mean you own a lake as well?'

'On the other side of the hill. I bought up all the land around it last year.'

'Sounds like a great idea.'

Half an hour later they were launching the canoe from a rickety old wharf at the head of the lake. Bullrushes speared the water; lily pads floated in the shallows. The lake itself basked under the noonday sun, the slow thrust and drip of the paddles scarcely disturbing the silence. They headed towards a small island cupped in a cove and beached the canoe. Niall lifted out the hamper. 'Hungry?'

Joss looked longingly at the water, where the ripples from their approach had already smoothed. 'I'm hot and dirty and I'd love a swim.'

'We swam once before, Joss—remember?'

She looked up at him and said quietly, 'I've never forgotten anything we did.'

His face was suddenly as naked to her as his sweat-streaked chest. 'Neither have I. Nor will I. Ever.'

Her eyes fell. *You'll know the right man*, her mother had always said. Niall felt as right to her now as he had six years ago; but in all good faith she had promised to marry someone else, and Niall would make no promises at all until he had passed his check-up. 'And will you remember today?' she cried with a bitterness that shocked her.

'Yes. You're part of my soul, Joss.'

She turned away in sudden anguish. She would hurt Bryan if she broke their engagement; but would she not hurt him more if she married him feeling the way she did about Niall?

She kicked off her sandals, ran into the water in her shorts and top, and plunged under the surface, trying to drown out Niall's image in the surge and hiss of the lake water. But as she surfaced and struck out from the shore, she was beginning to understand what had brought her here today; she had wanted to know if Niall was as real to her now as he had been six years ago.

Her wet clothes dragged at her body, slowing her down. The lake was cold. She trod water, watching Niall stroke past her in an energetic overarm crawl, knowing she already had her answer. Then she swam back to shore.

Her blouse was clammy against her back and her shorts were dripping; the air that had seemed so warm only a few minutes ago was cool now, making her shiver. Clambering awkwardly over the rocks on the shore, Joss edged behind some bushes until she was screened from the lake. Then she took off her outer garments, wringing the water from them. It was an act of courage to put them on again. Cursing herself for her own stupidity, she made her way back to the little beach. Niall was just emerging from the lake, shaking the water from his hair like a puppy. He was only wearing shorts. It's an unfair world, thought Joss sourly, and heard him call, 'Feels great, eh?'

'I'm freezing,' she said irritably and inaccurately.

'Take off your shorts and blouse and spread them over the bushes. They'll be dry by the time we've eaten.'

'I can't do that with you here,' she retorted.

'Joss, I promise I won't lay a finger on you.'

'I shouldn't be here at all!' she cried, feeling tears bite at her eyes. 'I'm engaged to someone else. It was wrong of me to come.'

Niall took her by the shoulders. 'Stop wallowing in guilt!' he snapped. 'Are we doing anything wrong?'

Her chin dropped to her chest. 'I shouldn't *be* here,' she whispered.

'But you are here.' He gave her a little shake. 'For whatever the reason, we've been given a day together—let's enjoy it.'

His remark touched her on the raw. She could feel her temper rising and made no effort to check it. 'Enjoy the present and to hell with tomorrow?' she said waspishly.

'One thing I learned when I was ill was to take each day as it comes.'

'But you're not ill now, and no one can live solely in the present—what of tomorrow, and tomorrow, and tomorrow? One week from today I'm to marry Bryan!'

Niall's fingers tightened with unconscious cruelty. 'Do you think I don't know that? If my check-up had been last week I'd be making love to you right now, Joss, fighting for you with every weapon I possess. But I can't do that. So I have to stand back and let you make up your own mind, even it that half-kills me.'

'You don't have to stand back!' she blazed. 'You could ask me to go to Boston with you and share in the results of the check-up, whatever they might be.'

'We've been through all this before!'

'Why was your mother's illness so hush-hush, Niall? Why did it change you?'

His face stilled. He said flatly, 'You've been talking to Clem.'

'Oh, Clem's like you—he's not about to give away any family secrets. Tell me about your mother, Niall.'

'No.'

'So you don't care if I marry Bryan on Saturday?'

Niall's features were as unyielding as the granite rocks Joss had hauled out of the ground. 'You've got to make up your own mind, Joss,' he said.

Leah had said more or less the same thing. Joss looked down at her wet blouse and knew she would keep it on, for how could she flaunt her body in front of this man who wanted so desperately to make love to her? Then Niall said evenly, 'This is difficult for you, Joss, I know. It's difficult because you're loyal and honest and true, and your agreement to marry Bryan wasn't a casual one.' His smile was wry. 'By some kind of convoluted reasoning I'd have thought the less of you if you'd broken your engagement the night we met at Scarlatti's.'

She gazed up at him dumbly and into her mind the three small words *I love you* lay as clear and limpid as the lake water over the rocks. She did not say them. She said, with a huge effort at restoring normality, 'I don't suppose Bryan would mind if we ate the picnic.'

So they did, seated on rocks in the sun, and afterwards paddled back to the gardens. When they were walking to the house Niall looked up the hill. 'Customers,' he remarked. 'Up by Clem's cabin.'

'Why does Clem live with you, Niall?'

'My father sold the family property two years ago and

moved into an apartment, so Clem had nowhere to go—he'd been with us for years as a general handyman. Now he works when he feels like it and complains the rest of the time . . . excuse me for a few minutes, will you, Joss?' After passing her the empty picnic basket, Niall jogged along the driveway towards the customers.

Joss carried the basket to the house, leaving it in the shade by the front door; Niall and the two customers had disappeared among the trees. She knew exactly what she was going to do. She walked up the hill, found Clem seated on his bench and said bluntly, 'Will you tell me where Niall's father lives?'

Clem took a tobacco pouch from his pocket and began rolling a cigarette. 'I might. Then again, I might not.'

The brown and white mongrel was still at Clem's feet, gazing at him adoringly. Stupid dog, thought Joss, and said, 'Do you enjoy being hard to get along with, Clem?'

He peered at her through eyebrows like unpruned hedges. 'Could be. Or else I'd just like to know what kinda stuff you're made of.'

'You're a manipulative and cantankerous old man,' she said sweetly. 'I want to find out about Niall's mother. He won't tell me. You won't tell me. His father is the logical person to ask.'

The cigarette, shreds of tobacco dangling from one end, was apparently completed. Clem began searching his pockets for matches. 'You never told me if you were gonna marry Niall.'

'I'm engaged to someone else,' she said tartly.

'Yeah? Get unengaged.'

'Only if you'll tell me where Niall's father lives.'

Clem sniggered uncouthly, lit the cigarette and exhaled a cloud of noxious blue smoke. 'Think you're pretty smart, eh?'

'Smart enough to know you'd like me and Niall to get

married,' Joss said slowly.

Clem shot her a disconcertingly shrewd glance. 'Not many people'd let me live with 'em,' he said. 'Niall took me in right away. You willin' to fight for him?'

She grinned. 'I'm standing here talking to you, aren't I?'

Clem puffed out another cloud of smoke. 'His dad lives in Vancouver. Montpelier Apartments on Straughan Avenue.'

Joss had not expected to win quite so easily. 'Thank you,' she gulped.

'Doubt that he'll let you past the door. Tight-lipped fella—like his son, only worse.'

'If I go all the way to Vancouver, he'd better let me past the door,' Joss said with a scowl.

'You better get rid of the other guy first. Look a little strange, otherwise.'

Joss had temporarily forgotten about Bryan. 'You're very fond of telling people what to do.'

'You should get back to the house, too. Unless you want Niall to know we bin havin' a cosy little chat.'

'I'm beginning to think Niall deserves a medal for having taken you in,' she said vigorously. 'Goodbye, Clem. *You* should quit smoking.'

'Keeps the flies away.' He winked at her. 'See you around.'

Fortunately Niall was still busy with the customers when Joss arrived back at the house. She put on his work boots again and trudged over to the garden, where she started the tiller and began ploughing the soil. There were a great many rocks, which gave her even more respect for the beauty Niall had created in the little valley. A few minutes later Niall came through the gap in the forsythia bushes that formed the garden's eastern boundary. Joss smiled at him.

'You've got mud on your face,' he said. 'Also on your knees and your shirt.'

'Also under my fingernails. Did you sell anything?'

'Four apple trees and two hundred strawberry plants. I might break even this year, having been in the red for the last four.'

'You've put a lot of money into the place.'

'I made a lot in my executive days. The rat race pays—that's why people stay in it.' Without altering his voice Niall added, 'You look absolutely right standing in my garden, Joss. You don't know how many times in the past four years I've pictured you here.'

Because the sun was at her back, Joss's face was in shadow. Perhaps this gave her courage. She heard herself say, 'Niall, do you love me?'

The sun in its turn exposed every nuance of feeling on his features. 'I wouldn't have thought you needed to ask that question.'

'I'm asking it.'

'Yes, I love you. I fell in love with you six years ago, and finding you again has simply confirmed it. I'll always love you, Joss.'

She tried to quench a happiness as golden as the petals on the forsythia. 'So your fear of illness goes very deep.'

'It's something I can't change.'

'Not even if you risk losing me again?'

His jaw was rigid. 'Are you going to marry Bryan?'

She said slowly, 'I'm not sure you have the right to ask that question, Niall.'

His eyes held hers. 'Then we'd better talk about something else, hadn't we?'

Strangely enough, although she knew she had been defeated, Joss was exhilarated by the battle. Her spine very straight, she said, 'I guess we had.'

'I not only love you, I like you,' he smiled.

'I can't imagine why,' she said demurely. 'A nag like me.'

'With mud on her face.' Niall stepped closer and wiped her cheekbone with his fingertip.

She could see the laughter in his eyes and felt his chest brush her shirt. He was standing close to her purposely, she knew; the mud on her face was only a pretext. 'Sex is not a fair weapon,' she said.

He widened his eyes in mock innocence. 'Am I kissing you with unbridled passion? Am I enticing you into the forsythia brushes to make love? Or worse, into the gooseberry patch? I think I'm behaving admirably under the circumstances.'

Disarmed, she said, 'I've always loved to see you laugh.'

'You've always been able to make me laugh.' He gave her the crooked smile she knew so well. 'The gooseberry bushes are starting to look very inviting, thorns and all—I think we should get back to work.'

She put her head to one side. 'How can I make you change your mind about Boston?'

'You can't. I learned certain lessons as a kid, Joss, and I can't unlearn them.'

'Won't.'

'Can't. But as soon as I get back from Boston, I'll court you as assiduously as I know how.' He raised one brow sardonically. 'Providing, that is, that you're not a married woman.'

Joss glowered at him. 'I hate it when you have the last word.'

He laughed. 'Why don't you use the tiller while I dump these rocks?'

They worked side by side for nearly two hours, by which time three-quarters of the bed had been tilled with peat moss and compost. Then Niall struck two large rocks. 'Have to use the mattock for these,' he grunted. 'Do you want to go up to the house, Joss, and bring back a couple of cold beers?'

'Great idea. Don't you get those out on your own, though—too hard on the back.'

He gave her a mock salute. 'No, Doc.'

'Today has been really good for me,' Joss said spontaneously. 'Last week was my first experience of a regular practice, so I wanted to do everything right—with the result that I was exhausted last night. Hauling rocks is great therapy.'

'Not everyone would see it that way . . . try not to trip over your toes on the way up to the house, huh?'

'Are you insinuating I can't fill your boots?'

Joss was smiling while she walked up to the house, and still smiling on her way back with two cans of beer. She came round the forsythia hedge, then stopped dead in her tracks. Niall was hunched over the tiller, clutching his side, his face contracted with pain.

He's ill again, she thought, and felt agony rip through her own body. I'm going to lose him. Oh, God, I can't bear it. Not again.

Then she started to run, the boots flopping on her feet. She dropped the beer cans on the ground at the edge of the garden and gasped, 'Niall, what's wrong?'

He was ashen-faced, half leaning against the handles of the tiller. 'Caught my hand between the rocks,' he muttered.

Only then did Joss take in the blood dripping between his fingers on to the sharp-edged boulders at his feet. In an immensity of relief that left her weak-kneed, she realised Niall had had an accident: nothing to do with his illness, nothing to do with his check-up. Instantly she became the calm, level-headed professional. She straightened out his left hand and assessed the damage, then said decisively, 'I'll run you to the nearest hospital—you'll need stitches and an X-ray to check for broken bones. You stay here and I'll back my car down.'

'Clem will take me.'

'*I* will take you.'

Incredibly Niall managed a smile. 'Yes, Doc.'

Joss covered the distance to the house in record time,

thrust her feet into her sandals and found a clean cloth in one of the kitchen drawers. When she got back to the garden she carefully wrapped Niall's injured hand in the cloth, then eased him into the car seat; he was leaning on her so heavily that she knew he was in shock. At the top of the hill she told Clem what had happened before driving down the lane towards the highway. 'Which is the nearest hospital, Niall?'

'Turn right. Right again at the next intersection. Hospital's in Stirling.'

His voice was thin with pain. She drove as fast as she could, found the red brick hospital with no trouble and ushered him in the door of the emergency department. He was whisked away by a very pretty nurse, and Joss was left to fill in the necessary forms and to wait.

She waited for nearly an hour, which gave her far too much time to think about that moment of sheer terror when she had first seen Niall bent over the tiller. Her visit today had more than achieved its purpose, she thought grimly. Niall was as real to her as he had ever been, and as right for her.

A white-coated attendant ushered Niall back into the waiting-room. Joss stood up, her eyes searching his face. He said rapidly, 'No broken bones, five stitches and a tetanus shot.'

There was a little colour in his cheeks and the lines of pain had eased from around his mouth. 'And you're chock-full of pain-killers,' she said.

He grinned. 'We could go dancing.'

'Not tonight,' she said firmly. 'I'm taking you straight home.'

'You sound just like the doctor,' he complained. But when they were seated in the car and the attendant had disappeared into the building he added quietly, 'I'm sorry I scared you, Joss. There was a moment when you dropped the beer cans that I thought you were one one who was going to pass out.'

'You weren't supposed to see that.'

'It was only an accident.'

Unwisely she stated the truth. 'For a moment I thought you were ill again—that the clock had gone back six years. That's why I looked so scared.'

He was silent for several seconds. Then he said, 'That proves my point, doesn't it—the high risk of being involved with me. That's why I'm not screaming at you to break your engagement.'

'It doesn't prove anything!' she cried. 'When you love someone there's risk involved—that's a fact of life.'

He did not pursue her use of the word love. 'Just take me home, will you, Joss?'

In swift compunction she said, 'We shouldn't be arguing, not now. I'll take you home and you're to go straight to bed.'

'Then I want you to leave,' he said inflexibly.

His words cut her to the quick. 'As Bryan's coming back tomorrow, I'd scarcely stay,' she said coldly, as she clashed the gears and drove out of the car park. They did not speak on the way home.

Clem was sitting on the front step of the house when they arrived; the two dogs circled the car, yapping at Joss's ankles, fawning around Niall's. Clem said acerbically, 'Caught your fingers between two rocks, eh? Dumb thing to do.'

Niall straightened, supporting his left wrist with his right hand. 'Not very bright,' he agreed.

'I ain't gonna be your nursemaid.'

'Good,' said Niall.

Clem pointed a dirty finger at Joss. 'She'll look after you—take you soup in bed.'

'Clem,' Niall said strongly, 'there are times when I can't stand the sight of you, and this is one of them. I'm going indoors to lie on the couch and Joss is going home.'

'To her fi-an-cey?' Clem sneered. 'You got blood in that hand, Niall Morgan, or apple juice?'

'Get lost!' Niall yelled.

'OK, OK, I c'n take a hint.' Clem whistled to the dogs. 'I'll be down later to check on the two of you,' he snickered, and shambled off up the hill.

'My father must have been a saint to have put up with him all those years,' Niall muttered. Then he turned to Joss. 'Thanks for your help, Joss. I'll be all right now.'

His blue eyes were as flat as his voice. She said clearly, 'I'm coming into the house to see you settled. I'll leave some food out for you and make a sling for your wrist. I shall then leave. I will not attempt to rape you.'

'Your eyes shoot little gold sparks when you're angry,' Niall remarked.

Her nostrils flared. 'Clem's got nothing on you! Get in the house, Niall Morgan, before you drop.'

The chesterfield, which was covered in old-fashioned chintz, was long enough to accommodate Niall. Joss stalked upstairs to his bedroom, a room that filled her with a confusion of emotions, grabbed a pillow and blanket from his bed and marched downstairs again. Scrupulously not touching him, she spread the blanket over his legs and put the pillow under his head. In the kitchen she mixed up some soup in a saucepan on the stove and made a couple of sandwiches, wrapping them in waxed paper and leaving them in the refrigerator. Then she went back into the living-room.

Niall was asleep. The drugs had done their work.

He had told her to leave; but she did not want to. Impulsively Joss knelt beside the chesterfield, resting her cheek on his chest, which was rising and falling with the slow rhythm of his breathing. She closed her eyes. She did not want to leave. She belonged here.

A hand was stroking her hair; her neck was cramped.

Joss opened her eyes. The room was almost dark, so dark that Niall's eyes were a smoky, mysterious grey. She nestled against his hand and said softly, 'I like that.'

'You were supposed to go home.'

'I didn't want to leave you.'

The darkness seemed to free him, for he said roughly, 'I'm glad you didn't . . . come here, Joss.'

She tried to get up, yelped from the pain in her knees, and sagged against the chesterfield again. 'Where's your sore hand?'

'Safely out of reach. Come closer, Joss.'

She eased herself beside him on the chesterfield, lying full-length, sliding an arm across his chest. The darkness enfolded them as he kissed her, his good arm pulling her almost on top of him with surprising strength, so that she was also enfolded in the warmth of his body. When he released her she said with a catch in her voice, 'I like that, too.'

'Amazing what one can accomplish with one arm.'

She giggled. 'How are you feeling?'

She could feel him smile in the darkness. 'Lousy,' he said succinctly. 'I think the needle's worn off.'

Joss was all doctor immediately. 'I'll get you a pill.'

'Lie still a minute—I'll survive,' he said lazily.

She relaxed, loving the tautness of his arm, the hard curve of his ribcage against her breast, the warmth of his throat by her cheek. She would be content to stay here for ever, she thought dreamily.

Then, with the crazy illogic of a dream, she heard Clem's cracked voice echo in her ear as if he was standing beside her in the room. 'You willin' to fight for him?' Clem had asked.

The dream collapsed; she could not stay for ever, not as things were, because Niall would not let her. To stay, she had to fight. And what better time than now? she realised in sudden excitement. Now, when Niall was holding her close and they were alone in the house. She would never be given a better one.

She said with the same lazy inflection as he, 'This is what it's all about, Niall. Being together—even though right now you're not feeling well. Holding on to each other in the dark.'

Along the length of her body she felt the tension gather in his. 'Joss, hush.'

'I can't.' She twisted, leaning her weight on one elbow so that she could discern his features. 'This is what love means to me . . . sharing the bad times as well as the good. There's nothing complicated or difficult about what we're doing, Niall—in fact, it's the most natural thing in the world.'

'Let it drop, Joss,' he said irritably. 'You know how I stand as far as the check-up's concerned—nothing's going to change my mind.'

She paused, marshalling her forces, which seemed pitifully inadequate against the iron wall of his will. 'What if your check-up went fine and we got married, and then a few years down the road you became ill again . . . would you abandon me?'

'That's a theoretical question—I can't answer that.'

'So you're a fair-weather lover.'

'Stop putting words into my mouth.'

'Niall, please let me go to Boston with you. Just so we can be together.'

'I have to go alone, Joss, I've told you that a dozen times.' He shifted on the chesterfield; she could feel his breath on her cheek. 'Look, my philosophy of life is very simple—we're born alone and we die alone. And you don't ask anyone else to share that dying.'

'I couldn't disagree more,' Joss cried. Her voice passionate with conviction, she made one last attempt. 'I told you about my brother Jake and his wife, didn't I? That's what love means to me, Niall—a sharing of the very worst life can throw at you . . . because two people are immeasurably stronger than one. That's the kind of marriage I want. I won't settle for less.'

Niall's voice was ice-cold. 'Then I have nothing to offer you.'

I've lost, Joss thought numbly. I tried, Clem. But he won't listen and I don't know what else to say . . . if only I can get out of here without bursting into tears. Please God, don't let me cry.

She swung her legs to the floor and stood up, desperately grateful for the darkness. 'I must go,' she said, her voice sounding as though it belonged to someone else. She added politely, 'Goodbye, Niall. I hope your hand will feel better tomorrow.'

He neither moved nor spoke. Searching for the doorway, Joss stumbled across the carpet. The hall was longer than she remembered. The front door opened smoothly and just as smoothly closed behind her, and her car was exactly where she had left it. She drove up the hill, past Clem's cabin, and down the tree-shrouded lane. At the bottom of the lane, where it widened, she stopped the car, leaned her arms on the steering wheel and wept.

She had been exiled from paradise.

CHAPTER TEN

WHEN JOSS woke from a leaden sleep the next morning to the shrill of the telephone bell, she thought for a moment that she was an intern again, back at the hospital on thirty-six-hour duty. Then she remembered Niall, and with a thrill of fear picked up the receiver. 'Hello,' she croaked.

'It's Magda. I've had a baby!'

Gamely Joss rose to the occasion. 'Congratulations! A boy or a girl? Did everything go well?'

'A girl, seven pounds four and a half ounces, and, if you want the truth, a funny-looking little thing,' said Magda joyfully. 'Charlie thinks she's beautiful. When are you coming to see us?'

Joss peered at her clock. Six-thirty. 'Seven?' she ventured.

'I know it's awfully early, but I'm so excited I'm calling everyone I know. My mum and dad are flying up tomorrow. We made grandparents out of them—imagine that! As for Charlie,' Magda added complacently, 'he says nothing he could ever invent would approach the perfection of the baby. We've been arguing about names. He favours Greek mythology and I go for Hollywood stars—but we've both agreed on Jocelyn for her second name.'

'That's very sweet of you.'

'Hurry up and see your namesake!'

So Joss hurried, and at ten past seven was admitted into Magda's room. Charlie was holding the baby, his face a huge, seraphic smile, while Magda was propped up against the pillows. Magda talked for ten minutes without stopping, pointing out all the marvels of the baby's form, from her wrinkled little face to the minuteness of her toenails. Then she said generously, 'You can hold her if you like . . . OK, Charlie?'

Charlie's razor-keen mind seemed to have forgotten that Joss was a graduate in medicine who had delivered a number of babies. 'Be careful, Joss, she's very tiny,' he admonished. 'Have you got her head? It's very important to support her head . . . there you go.' With some reluctance he relinquished the baby.

The tiny head with its fuzz of brown hair fitted neatly under Joss's chin; the baby seemed almost weightless. Filled with tenderness and with an incredible wonder for new life, which no medical textbook could adequately explain, Joss sat very still. The baby gave a little snort, as of complete boredom. Joss chuckled with delight.

'You look just fine holding a baby,' Magda remarked. 'Doesn't she, Charlie? Time you had one of your own, Joss.'

Joss gaped at her friend. What if this were her child? The father could not possibly be Bryan. The only man to give her a child had to be Niall. She said over-loudly, 'I'm going to break my engagement, Magda.'

'Thank goodness,' said Magda.

'What do you mean, thank goodness?' Joss bristled. 'Don't you like Bryan?'

'Of course I do—he's a fine, upstanding citizen. But Niall's the man for you, not Bryan. You're so loyal, Joss, with all those old-fashioned virtues—I was terrified you'd marry Bryan just because you'd promised to.'

'Oh,' said Joss weakly. 'Well, I won't. I'll have to tell him this afternoon when he comes home from Switzerland. What on earth will I say?'

'You'll think of something,' Magda said heartlessly. 'Can I have the baby now? Charlie wants to call her Thea or Thalia or even Diantha, can you imagine that?'

'While you'd call her Sissy or Meryl,' Joss teased. 'Well, there's always Venus. Or Cher.'

She had the dim feeling she ought not to be joking on the day when she was going to break her engagement. But the open acknowledgement of a decision that had been brewing ever since the night at Scarlatti's had filled her with relief and a lightness of spirit. It was the right decision. The only decision. While Bryan would be hurt, he would be hurt a great deal more were she to marry him when she was in love with someone else.

I'm in love with Niall, she thought, carefully handing the baby over to Magda. I've loved him since the first moment I saw him at the Red Lion, and I always will love him. I don't know if we'll ever be together. But I do know I can't marry anyone else.

Which, for now, was enough.

When Bryan's plane arrived at three that afternoon, Joss was waiting at the barricade outside Customs. She had chosen to wear a plainly cut navy blue dress with a white collar and cuffs, for it seemed to suit her mood: relief had been usurped by panic.

Bryan was one of the first through Customs. He was wearing one of his innumerable pinstripe suits which gave him such an air of distinction, and his smile when he saw her was uncharacteristically wide. He was not a man to indulge in public displays of affection, but before she could turn her cheek he had kissed her firmly on the lips. 'Wonderful to see you, Joss. I missed you. You're looking very—er—regal.'

She managed a smile. 'Hello, Bryan.'

'One week from today you'll be my wife.'

A little girl tripped over Joss's foot, and the frantic mother pushed through the crowd to grab her. It did not seem an opportune time for Joss to explain that she was not going to marry him. Instead she gulped, 'Let's get out of here.'

'Good idea. The conference was marvellous, I've got so much to tell you.'

The conference, fortunately, lasted them all the way to Bryan's apartment; he lived in a luxury flat near the hospital. Joss carried in his briefcase. Bryan dumped his suitcase on the floor, closed the door and said, 'Come here, Joss.'

His words were an uncanny echo of Niall's. In a brittle voice Joss said, 'Bryan, I'm terribly sorry, but I can't marry you.'

He dropped his keys on the very beautiful ormolu table by the door; the noise seemed shockingly loud. 'Would you mind saying that again?'

'I can't marry you,' she repeated, and because she was so nervous she sounded unfeeling.

'Are you going to marry Niall?'

'No.' Bravely she met Bryan's eyes. 'But I still love him, Bryan. I guess in a way I never stopped, and then when I saw him again . . . I'm so *sorry*, but I can't marry you, it wouldn't be fair to either of us, and why does everything I say sound like a Victorian novel?'

Her hands were clasped in front of her, the knuckles as white as her cuffs. Bryan took her hands in his, saying evenly, 'Are you sure about this? I know it was a shock to meet him again—maybe we should delay the wedding until you're more used to the idea that he's still around.'

'I'm sure.'

He rubbed her wrists, which were as rigid as steel bars, and with a shock she realised that he was not completely surprised by her decision. She muttered, 'You were expecting this, weren't you?'

'I guess so. Perhaps it was one of the reasons I didn't call you from Switzerland—I wasn't sure what I'd hear.'

Although Bryan was doing a good job of hiding his emotions, she knew him well enough to discern the hurt beneath his reserve. 'I feel dreadful,' she whispered. 'I thought I loved you, Bryan. But this other . . . it's like a force of nature. I can't help it, it's bigger than me.'

'I only hope he'll make you happy,' Bryan said stiffly.

She did not want to talk about Niall's one-sided view of love. 'Will you tell your mother?' she asked.

'I'll go and see her. But I know she'll want to see you as well; she's very fond of you, Joss.'

So eight o'clock that evening found Joss opening the door of her apartment to Leah. Leah embraced her and said forthrightly, 'I know this hasn't been easy for you, but you've made absolutely the right decision, Joss. I'd have been very upset if you'd married my son when you were in love with someone else.'

'I hurt Bryan, though.'

'I don't want to belittle his emotions. But Bryan loves his work, and once the fuss about the wedding has died down he'll find great comfort in that. Now,' she went on briskly, 'we have a lot to do. I'd suggest you put a notice in the newspaper tomorrow announcing that the wedding has been cancelled. I brought a list of the out-of-town guests with me, we could split those between us and phone them. Then there's the minister, the organist, the florists, and the caterers at the hotel. You can probably return your dress. Bryan said he'd look after the condominium lease and cancel the arrangements for the honeymoon.'

Joss had paled under this onslaught. 'I've got a room full of gifts, too,' she said.

'They'll all have to be returned.'

'Do you think people sometimes get married because cancelling the wedding is too complicated?'

'I wouldn't be surprised.' Leah gave Joss a sideways smile. 'I'm glad you're not one of them.'

The next three days long remained in Joss's memory. After the first two or three phone calls she evolved a formula for announcing the cancellation of her wedding, and became more adept at fielding the inevitable awkward questions. The minister tried to turn her call into a counselling session, which she ended by announcing that she was in love with someone else; the organist was pleased because it meant he could go to his cottage for the weekend. She forfeited a huge deposit at the caterers and a lesser one at the florists. She returned her white silk suit. Only then did she turn her attention to the spare bedroom, where each gift would have to be rewrapped with a note enclosed. After buying quantities of brown paper, string and tape, Joss set to work.

On Wednesday morning, when the pile was considerably depleted, she came to the box containing the ceramic cherubs and the bunch of grapes; the cherubs were still smirking indefatigably. Quite suddenly Joss found herself with her hands pressed to her eyes and tears spurting from between her fingers. She was so glad to be getting rid of the cherubs and yet she felt so guilty about breaking her engagement.

Bryan had been weighing heavily on her mind. They had had to meet the day before to sign the condominium release form, a meeting which had excoriated Joss's spirits, for although Bryan had been very much on his dignity, he had let it be known that he was not sleeping well and had lost five pounds; she would have felt better had he thrown the release form at her and called her a heartless bitch. She herself was not sleeping well, either. She had not informed Niall of her broken engagement, for what was the use? He would not take her to Boston or allow her the intimacy she craved, and she knew from experience it was useless to beg for either one.

Wednesday afternoon she took the last box to the post office, spent an hour at the clinic and then visited Magda, who was home with the baby. The baby had been named Diana Jocelyn. 'Diana after the princess and the goddess of the hunt,' Madga said triumphantly.

'Charlie says Artemis is the proper Greek name, but I drew the line at that. Joss, you look awful.'

Joss picked up Nasturtium and buried her face in the cat's fur, trying to hide the fact that she was on the brink of tears again. 'I'm tired, that's all. People are funny when you break an engagement—some of them talk in a hushed voice as if you'd died, and others ask all kinds of rude questions. I'm not sure which is worse.'

'Why don't you go away for a few days?'

'Oh, I couldn't leave the clinic.'

'Joss, you've hired a very competent contractor to remodel the clinic, and you were going away on your honeymoon next week, anyway. Bermuda, wasn't it? So go away a bit earlier, that's all.'

'But——'

'You don't have to go to Bermuda!' Magda said, exasperated. 'Go home and see your parents, or go to New York and spend lots of money on Fifth Avenue. But get out of Toronto.'

'That's a good idea,' Joss said slowly. 'You see, I keep hoping Niall will call, even though I know he's not going to.'

'He's a damned fool.'

Joss looked up, more life in her face than she had shown all week. 'I could go to Vancouver,' she exclaimed. 'If I talked to his father, I might understand Niall better. Magda, you're a genius!'

'Charlie's the genius,' Magda grinned. 'I've just got common sense. One of your sisters lives in Vancouver, doesn't she?'

'Blanche—I could stay with her. I'll book my ticket as soon as I get home.'

'You can't go home until you've admired Diana.'

It was no hardship to admire Diana, who was sleeping very peacefully for a child who, according to her mother, had astoundingly active lungs. Joss went straight home afterwards, and after two phone calls had a flight out at six o'clock the next morning which would be met by Blanche. She threw some clothes in a suitcase that night, and with a feeling of genuine escape left her apartment at four-thirty the next morning.

One of her first actions in Vancouver was to look up Niall's father's telephone number. But although she tried at different hours each day, she did not get an answer until Monday. The weekend had been pleasant enough, shopping and chatting with Blanche, and lying in the sun in her sister's beautiful garden; the wedding that should have taken place on Saturday seemed very remote. But the thought of Niall nagged at Joss continually. Would he know by now that she had not married Bryan? Or would he even have checked? Was he worried about his trip to Boston? Even, on a more minor scale, had his hand healed? She did not know the answer to any of these questions, nor could she go home to ask them; until she reached Niall's father she was in limbo.

On Monday morning the telephone was lifted on the second ring. A very precise male voice said, 'Gerald Morgan speaking.'

Overwhelmed by relief, Joss was glad she had rehearsed her lines. She said pleasantly, 'Mr Morgan, my name is Jocelyn MacDougall. I'm a good friend of your son Niall; we first met six years ago.' She crossed her fingers behind her back, for she had decided to tell an untruth to strengthen her case. 'When Niall knew I was coming to Vancouver to visit my sister, he asked me to phone you and invite myself to tea.' She gave a charming little laugh. 'I hope you don't think that's too forward of me. Clem asked to be remembered to you, as well.'

'Ah, yes, Clem.' Gerald Morgan cleared his throat. 'When would be a convenient time for you, Miss MacDougall?'

'Would this afternoon be too soon?'

'Not at all. Shall we say four o'clock? You know the address?'

'Thank you, yes. I'll see you then.'

She rang off and uncrossed her fingers. One hurdle was cleared. Now all she had to do was persuade a man who sounded like no fool and who had a reputation for being close-mouthed to talk about the illness of his long-dead wife.

She wore the navy dress with the white collar and cuffs, minimal make-up, and carried a small bunch of freesias as a gift. The apartment building overlooked Stanley Park and the mountains, and reeked of opulence; a place more different than the Nova Scotia farm would be hard to imagine. With a sinking heart Joss gave her name to the uniformed security guard and was eventually permitted to tap across the marble-floored foyer to the brass-doored lifts. Mr Morgan's suite was on the tenth floor, where her shoes now sank into a plush pink carpet. Trying to take courage from the memory of Niall stripped to the waist in the garden, she pressed the bell and, because of the peephole, composed her face. The door swung open.

All her carefully prepared speeches were forgotten. Joss said naïvely, 'You're so like your son! I would have known you anywhere,' and gave Gerald Morgan the full benefit of her smile.

She was a very beautiful young woman. Gerald Morgan pressed her hand and said, 'Do come in, Miss MacDougall. It is Miss MacDougall? Or do you prefer Ms?' He made the latter abbreviation sound in questionable taste.

Joss had recovered a little. 'It's Dr MacDougall, actually,' she said smoothly. 'I'm starting up a medical practice in Toronto this summer.'

'Really?' He gave a dry laugh. 'In my day such a charming girl as yourself would not have been exposed to the unpleasant realities of a medical career.'

Her smile did not waver. 'I'm sure you see the changes as an improvement, Mr Morgan.' Holding out the tissue-wrapped freesias, she added, 'To thank you for your kind invitation.'

Very briefly a sly humour lurked in the blue eyes that once must have been the deep blue of Niall's. 'In my day the men gave the flowers to the women . . . another improvement. Please take a seat, Dr MacDougall, and I shall bring in the tea.'

The window had a breathtaking view of the harbour and the mountains and the chair was a highly uncomfortable antique. Joss sat very straight, crossing her ankles, and when Mr Morgan brought in a silver tea service, putting it on the hand-carved table between the two chairs, she took the opportunity to study him. Gerald Morgan's likeness to Niall was more a matter of height and bone-structure than personality, for whereas Niall crackled with vitality, Gerald Morgan seemed dessicated, his smile rarely used, his emotions well hidden. After he had poured the tea into exquisite bone china cups, he offered her a choice of lemon or milk and passed her a plate of tiny cakes. Then he said politely, 'You mentioned that you've known Niall for six years. You're too young to have been one of his medical attendants, surely?'

Joss balanced the cake on her embroidered serviette, whose creases were knife-sharp, and decided to use shock tactics. 'I only completed my internship a couple of months ago,' she said. 'The summer I met Niall I was singing in a downtown pub in Toronto.'

'Indeed.'

Gerald Morgan could make one word express a great deal. 'Indeed,' she said agreeably. 'We knew each other for four days. We fell in love, Mr Morgan.'

He leaned back in his chair and crossed his legs. 'I do not believe I have ever heard my son mention your name.'

'I would be surprised if he had.' Joss discovered that she was enjoying herself, for in Gerald Morgan she had found a worthy opponent. 'Niall vanished after four days, having told me he had a wife.'

'A palpable lie,' Mr Morgan murmured.

'Quite inadvertently I discovered that instead of being married, Niall was, or so he believed, terminally ill. I tried to trace him but I was unsuccessful. The tragedy was that he had not seen fit to tell me the truth.'

The faded blue eyes did not respond to her challenge. 'Once cured, did he then trace you?'

'He tried—but he only knew my stage name. So for five years I believed him to be dead.'

'Dear me,' said Mr Morgan.

Joss stifled a swift surge of anger and said calmly, 'I have a second confession to make—apart from being in love with your son, I mean. Niall has no idea I'm in Vancouver. I came here today entirely on my own accord.'

'Your character begins to intrigue me, Dr MacDougall.'

'Do my motives intrigue you, Mr Morgan?'

'I am sure you will reveal them in time.'

'Indeed,' she said drily. 'I met Niall quite by chance in a restaurant nearly three weeks ago, and it soon became obvious that our feelings for each other had not changed.'

'So am I to congratulate you?'

'No.' Letting the single word hang in the air, Joss took a sip of her tea.

'Perhaps you are mistaken in my son's feelings?'

'Your son refuses to commit himself to me until he has passed his final medical in Boston. His appointment is later this week.'

'A very sensible decision.'

'No, Mr Morgan—a very bad decision. Six years ago Niall vanished because he couldn't share the facts of his

illness with me. He is, in effect, doing the same thing
again. If his check-up is OK, sure, he'll marry me. But if
it's not—forget it. You won't see Niall for dust.' Joss
leaned forward, her gold-flecked eyes fierce with
emotion. 'I came here today to find out why.'

'My son and I are not close, Dr MacDougall.'

'Niall's mother—your wife—died after a long illness.
Clem would tell me very little, but he did say Niall
changed during the course of that illness. Why, Mr
Morgan?'

There were patches of colour in Gerald Morgan's
lined cheeks. 'That is a question you have no right to
ask.'

She gave him a disarming smile. 'I have every right to
ask—I'm in love with your son, Mr Morgan.'

'You'd run him round in circles,' Gerald Morgan said
pettishly.

Her laugh was a genuine, delightful cascade of sound.
'Niall? You don't know him very well!'

'No, I don't.'

Joss would have had to be deaf not to have heard the
bitterness in the precise voice. 'You could, though—it's
never too late,' she said with deep conviction. 'Mr
Morgan, I'm quite sure you think that I'm a brash and
horribly modern young woman with no inkling of her
proper place . . . and I'm now going to make matters
worse by giving you my theory. I think you kept your
wife's illness—and I have no idea of its nature—hidden
from Niall. Tucked away. Out of sight. Because of that,
I believe it assumed far too much importance to him,
while simultaneously he was taught no skills to deal with
it. I believe that ever since then he has been afraid of
illness, and that's why he won't marry me before his
check-up.'

'Brash is too mild a word,' Gerald Morgan said
sharply.

She refused to back down. 'Try honest.'

'So you would marry him, even knowing he was ill?'

'Yes. I love him, you see. For better, for worse.'

'Niall hated to discuss his illness with me. But being a doctor, you might know what the worst can entail.'

'I am not making the choice out of ignorance, but out of love,' said Joss.

Gerald Morgan turned his head to gaze out of the window; his profile reminded Joss so strongly of his son's that she was suddenly faint with longing for Niall. In an expressionless voice Niall's father said, 'You are quite correct in your assumptions. I did keep Sylvia's illness a secret from Niall.'

Joss sat very still. She said gently, 'What was wrong with her?'

He was still staring out of the window. 'Today it would be called Alzheimer's, I believe. She became forgetful and disorientated. She would wander the streets and be unable to tell anyone her name, and the police would have to bring her back. Twice she nearly set the house on fire by putting food to cook on the stove and then leaving it . . . how could I share all this with a young boy?' Not waiting for an answer, he went on, 'She got worse. At times she was paranoid, and you'd find her cowering in the wardrobe. Other days she became frighteningly aggressive—I hid all the knives and kept the tools locked up. Sometimes she'd even throw off her clothes and yell obscenities at me . . . my beautiful, gentle Sylvia.' He looked directly at Joss, dry-eyed. 'I kept her hidden from Niall as much as I could, yes. How could I share with him what I could not bear myself . . . the woman I loved changing into another woman who was a stranger to me'.

His back was rigid; but his hands were trembling very lightly as he reached for his teacup. Her heart aching for him, Joss said, 'I understand—it must have been terrible for you.'

With more emotion that he had yet shown he said, 'I

was *glad* when she died. How could I tell Niall that?'

'I do understand,' Joss repeated helplessly.

'I believe you do.' Gerald Morgan inclined his head in a courtly gesture. 'My son is a fortunate man.'

Joss led him on to talk more about his marriage, until the vivid images of a crazed Sylvia were replaced by happier images of earlier times. She told him how she had broken her engagement to Bryan, and when she spoke of Niall she allowed all her love to shine in her face. Then she looked at her watch. 'I've overstayed my welcome,' she said. 'Thank you, Mr Morgan—you've been more than kind.'

He stood up and formally shook her hand. 'It has been my pleasure. I would like to think that you might be the catalyst to bring Niall and myself closer together . . . I trust this will be the first of many meetings.'

With all her heart Joss hoped the same. She left the apartment, went back to Blanche's, and was lucky enough to get a booking on the first flight east the next morning. Partly because of her training, partly instinctively, she had been able to fill in the details of Gerald Morgan's bleak little narrative. To a young boy, an only child, the changes in his mother must have been terrifying, doubly so because they were shrouded in secrecy. No wonder illness loomed so large in Niall's imagination; no wonder he felt he could not expose Joss to the kind of suffering he himself had gone through.

Somehow, and she had no idea how, she had to change this view.

CHAPTER ELEVEN

AT FOUR-THIRTY the next afternoon, Toronto time, Joss was walking up the front steps of her apartment building. She felt stale and tired, and not nearly as sanguine that anything she could do would change Niall's mind.

The superintendent, who was middle-aged, overweight and unfailingly glum, was vacuuming the entrance hall. Joss summoned up a smile and said brightly, 'Good afternoon, Mr Garner.'

He did not smile back. 'Do you know someone called Niall Morgan?' he said suspiciously.

Her hand tensed on her suitcase. 'Yes.'

'He said you did. But I knew you were engaged to that doctor with the black car.'

Panic-stricken, Joss asked, 'Is anything wrong?'

He smiled sourly. 'You've got an apartment full of dead flowers, that's all that's wrong.'

She plunked her suitcase on the floor. 'What are you talking about?'

'He came here on Friday looking for you, that Niall Morgan. Said he'd been phoning your apartment and you weren't answering, maybe you were ill. I finally had to tell him you were away, only way to get him off my back.' Mr Garner made a couple of unenthusiastic passes with the vacuum cleaner.

'What's that got to do with dead flowers?' Joss said blankly, wondering if jet travel had affected her mind.

'He came back that afternoon with all these flowers. He wanted to put them in your apartment, but I told him that was against the rules.' Mr Garner leaned on the

172

handle of the vacuum cleaner, his brow furrowing in unaccustomed thought. 'Hard guy to say no to. First thing you know, I'd let him into your apartment. I stayed with him the whole time, mind you, I didn't let him out of my sight,' he added righteously. 'But that was Friday and here it is Tuesday. You're kind of late as far as those flowers are concerned.' He sniffed. 'Left you a letter, too, he did. Funny way for a guy to behave when you're going to marry someone else.'

'I'm not,' said Joss with an incandescent smile. 'Maybe I'm going to marry him instead.' She suddenly grabbed the superintendent and waltzed him around in a circle. 'You've made my day, Mr Garner!'

'That's nice,' Mr Garner said dourly, detaching himself as fast as he could. 'You better get the flowers in the garbage before the truck comes—and don't forget your suitcase.'

Joss had been rushing for the lift. She ran back, picked up her case, gave him another dazzling smile and hurried back to the lift, which then seemed to take forever to reach her floor. She was so excited she had trouble fitting the key in the lock of her door. But finally she pushed it open and walked in.

The apartment smelled of dead flowers. The living-room table was a veritable forest of wilting apple blossoms, tarnished forsythia, and drooping roses. A large white envelope bearing her name was prominently displayed in front of the foremost bouquet of roses. They had been, in their prime, red roses. Joss kicked the door shut behind her and tore open the envelope.

Across the single sheet of paper in an untidy but very masculine sprawl was written, 'Darling Joss, will you marry me? Niall.'

Joss sat down hard on the nearest chair and burst into tears.

Although they were tears of happiness, it took her two or three minutes to stop their flow, and not until then did she turn the paper over and check the inside of the envelope. Nothing else. Not a word of explanation, not even the date that the letter had been written. Just that one, simple question to which she already knew the answer.

Pushing back the chair, Joss hurried to the telephone and dialled Niall's number. After eight rings she broke the connection, then dialled again. No answer. He was out in the garden, she thought in frustration. She had to see him. She couldn't wait.

Taking the letter with her, because otherwise she was afraid she might think she had dreamed the whole episode, she took the lift to the basement and started her car. The traffic was heavy heading out of the city, so it was after six when she turned into the leafy lane and drove past Clem's cabin. Clem was not in sight. But the gardens were spread out before her in their order and beauty, and she knew she had come home.

She checked the house first. Both the front and back doors were locked and no one answered either bell. Biting her lip, Joss walked around the front of the house again. Bees hummed among the rock plants and the wind sighed drowsily in the birches. But that was all. She could not hear the tiller or the tractor, or even the sound of voices.

She drove around the rest of the property, searching for Niall's tall figure in the fields and orchards. She even checked the wharf, where the canoe was tipped, keel up. Slowly she drove back up the hill towards Clem's cabin. Niall's check-up, she was almost sure, was the day after tomorrow. She had not expected that he would already have left.

Clem was at the crest of the hill, slouched over a wheelbarrow, a dog at each heel. Joss braked and called out of the window, 'Where's Niall, Clem?'

'Boston.'

'Oh, damn,' she said unhappily. 'When did he leave?'

'Yesterday. His appointment got put forward.'

'When will he be back?'

Clem shrugged. 'Dunno. He said he'd call.'

'You didn't answer the phone this afternoon,' she said snappishly.

'I don't answer nuthin' after five o'clock,' Clem announced.

Her shoulders sagged. 'I don't even know where he is in Boston,' she said, and with a chill of superstitious fear remembered her hopeless search in Toronto six years ago.

'You bin away?' Clem asked.

'Yes,' she said absently, drumming on the wheel with her fingers, wondering how long it would take her to contact every hospital in Boston. She wanted to be with Niall. Now. He needed her, she was sure of it.

'You see his dad?'

'Niall's father? Yes, I did. I found out everything I wanted to know.'

'You did?'

There was a new note in Clem's voice, one she had not heard before: respect. Even in her distress Joss felt a quiver of inner amusement. 'Yes,' she said artlessly. 'He told me all about his wife's illness.'

'Didja hold a gun to his head?'

She ticked off her fingers. 'I lied to him on the telephone and then confessed that I'd lied. I told him I used to sing in a pub. And I told him that I love his son.'

Clem gave one of his uncouth cackles of laughter. The brown and white mongrel wagged its tail. Then Clem fished in one of the deep pockets of his dungarees, which Joss would swear had not been washed since the last time she saw him, and produced a ring of keys. 'The gold key'll unlock the front door. Maybe he left the name of the hotel lyin' around. Or else you could call his local doctor. Edward Stairs. He likely could tell you where Niall is.'

She seized the keys in case Clem changed his mind and said pertly, 'You must approve of me, Clem.'

'You'll do. You get unengaged yet?'

'Yes.' Her mouth quirked. 'I might even be re-engaged. I'll let you know what I'm doing about Boston on my way out.'

The house was cool and tidy and felt very empty. The downstairs yielded no clues. But when Joss went upstairs and walked into Niall's bedroom, she immediately saw a typed official letter beside the telephone on the bedside table. The letter was from a Boston physician and named the times and places of Niall's various appointments. The final one was at one o'clock the next afternoon.

Joss sat down on the bed, her hand smoothing the covers with a peculiar sense of intimacy. She wanted to be with Niall when he went for that appointment. Whatever the result, her place was at his side.

There was a telephone book in the drawer of the bedside table. She booked a seat on the only available flight to Boston the next morning, that would get her in at quarter to twelve, put down the phone wondering how she was going to pay for all this junketing around the country, and discovered that she did not care. Taking off her shoes she lay down on the bed. The pillow smelled elusively of Niall's aftershave. A little smile on her lips, she closed her eyes.

A bell was ringing and a hoarse voice calling her name. Joss sat up, realising the voice was Clem's. This was the second time she had fallen asleep in Niall's house, she thought in confusion, trying to smooth the indentation of her head from his pillow. 'I'll be right down!' she called.

In the hallway Clem peered at her from beneath his bushy brows. 'Figured you'd fallen down the cellar steps,' he said bellicosely.

'What's the time?'

'Nigh on eight-thirty.'

'I—I fell asleep,' she said lamely.

'And you weren't using the guest room,' Clem sniggered. 'Time you two got hitched.'

Joss said loftily, 'You have a dirty mind, Clem. I'm flying to Boston tomorrow morning.'

He grinned at her; his teeth would have been an impecunious dentist's dream. 'Smart move.'

'I'm glad you approve,' she said and added incautiously, 'I'd better go home and unpack one suitcase before I pack the next.'

'You figurin' on stayin' over, eh?'

She blushed, said loudly, 'Will you lock up the house again, please?' and passed him the keys. The dogs were sitting patiently on the front step; they paid her no attention whatsoever as she got in her car and drove away.

The flight to Boston was fifteen minutes late because of head winds; there was a queue at the taxi stand, and the air was hot and humid. In the tall plate-glass windows Joss could see her own reflection, that of a composed young woman in a red skirt and a loose jacket splashed with big red flowers. She did not feel composed. She was a mass of nerves. Which was not a medically accurate term, she reproved herself.

The taxis came and went, the queue grew shorter and the hands of the clock crept around its circumference. She had not brought a suitcase after all, for to prepare for an overnight stay seemed to be tempting fate. Superstition was not medically acceptable either, she thought glumly. Finally the taxi that drew up was her own. She gave the driver the doctor's address and said she was in a hurry.

He took her at her word, racing yellow lights and swearing at unwary pedestrians. But he delivered her by quarter to one at a brick and glass tower that housed several medical clinics; Joss tipped him generously, pushed through the swing doors and was enveloped in the artificial chill of air-conditioning.

'I'm looking for Dr Mappin's office,' she said to the girl at the information desk.

'Eleventh floor, turn right, suite sixteen.'

The lift was computerised, and so quiet that Joss was afraid the other occupants would hear the pounding of her heart. She got off on the eleventh floor and turned right. The door to suite sixteen was closed. For a long moment she stood outside, trying to calm herself. Then she opened the door.

The doctor's office was painted a soothing shade of rose pink with an attractive display of plants and a seemingly casual arrangement of chairs and magazine tables; the doctor in Joss was taking mental notes for her own clinic, even while the woman in her was seeking out Niall. There were three people waiting in the office. Of the three, only Niall had his back to her.

The receptionist at the brightly lit counter said, 'Kindly shut the door, madam. May I help you?' She reminded Joss very strongly of Mr Garner.

Joss swallowed. 'I'm here with Mr Morgan,' she said, and hoped she was telling the truth.

Niall turned his head, dropped his magazine and stood up, looking thunderstruck. '*Joss* . . . how did you get here?'

'A plane,' she said intelligently.

'The superintendent didn't know when you'd be back—I never expected to see you here.'

In sudden panic she said, 'Maybe I shouldn't have come.'

He closed the space between them and took her in his arms. 'Don't be ridiculous,' he said, and kissed her at some length.

She kissed him back, briefly forgetting all her other

concerns in the joy of his embrace. Her body seemed to fit the circle of his arms; he was kissing her like a man in love. When he released her, they spoke simultaneously.

'Did you——' he said.

'How have——' she began.

He laughed. 'You first.'

'How have your tests gone?'

'OK. But I'll be glad when this is over.'

She was close enough to see the lines of strain in his face, and reached up a hand to smooth his cheek. 'I'm glad I'm here,' she said simply.

His hug was bone-cracking. 'Oh, God, so am I—I was an idiot, Joss, to try and keep you away. Did you get my letter?'

'Dr Mappin will see you now, Mr Morgan,' said the receptionist.

Joss turned in the circle of Niall's arms; the woman looked as disapproving as if Joss and Niall had been making love on the rose-pink carpet. Ignoring the receptionist, all his attention on the woman in his arms, Niall said, 'Joss, will you come in with me?'

She, of all people, knew the significance of that question. She took his hand and said gravely, 'Thank you.' The receptionist sniffed.

Dr Mappin rose to his feet when they entered his office, which was adorned with two very fine paintings and an antique mahogany desk; not, thought Joss, quite the right ambience for Queen Street West. The doctor was older than she had expected, with immensely kind brown eyes. He raised his brows a little when he saw her.

Niall said, 'Dr Mappin, I'd like you to meet my——' He stopped in mid-sentence. 'Joss, you didn't answer my question. *Did* you get my letter? Will you marry me?'

'Yes and yes,' she said, her heart in her eyes. 'Although I shall insist on some fresh roses.'

'Sweetheart, you shall have acres of them,' Niall said exultantly. He then completed the introduction more moderately. 'Dr Mappin, I'd like you to meet my fiancée, Dr Jocelyn MacDougall, from Toronto.'

'Delighted, Dr MacDougall.' Transferring his attention to Niall, Dr Mappin said, 'I have a wedding gift for you —you're in perfect health, Mr Morgan. Congratulations.'

Joss was standing close enough to Niall to sense an infinitesimal release of tension. 'I don't have to come back?' Niall said quietly.

Dr Mappin gave him a broad smile. 'I never want to see you again,' he joked. 'You did a very brave thing five years ago, and I'm extremely happy with the results.'

Niall gave his head a little shake. 'I can't quite take it in,' he said.

'I've left copies of all the reports _with the receptionist; you might want to take them with you.' Dr Mappin talked briefly of a few technical matters, then smiled at both of them. 'May I wish you every happiness in your married life.'

The appointment was over. Joss ushered Niall out of the office, picked up the file at the desk and walked with him to the elevator. It was crowded, as was the pavement outside the medical building. The heat struck at them and the snarl of traffic assaulted their ears. Niall looked around him as if he was not quite sure where he was. 'This is crazy—I figured I'd be dancing for joy if all the reports were OK,' he said. 'Instead I just feel kind of numb inside.'

Joss took his hand. 'You've lived with fear for six years,' she said. 'You can't expect to do a complete turnabout in five minutes.'

He was looking around him like an animal trapped in a cage. 'I was going to paint the town red. Or at least a shade of pink. Now all I want to do is get the hell out of here.' He squeezed her fingers, looking into her eyes with desperate intensity. 'Don't get me wrong, Joss—I've never been so happy to see anyone in my life as I was to see you when you walked into the doctor's office. I'd marry you five minutes from now if it were legally possible, and I want to make love to you so badly it hurts. But . . . not here. Not in this city.'

She understood completely. Six years ago when Niall had submitted himself to all the risks of an experimental drug he had suffered here; and all his check-ups, those times of uncertainty and dread, had taken place here as well. Boston was not a city of happy memories for Niall; and she too wanted to break free of the past's tyrannical hold. She said calmly, 'We'll go to the airport and get on a plane. We can go anywhere we like.'

Niall put his arms around her waist, almost lifting her off her feet. 'Joss, you're a marvel,' he said.

He hailed a cab and they drove first to his hotel to get his luggage, and then to the airport. They held hands the whole way and talked very little. Inside the terminal Niall stopped twenty feet from the Air Canada ticket counter. 'I don't want to go home—not yet,' he said. 'Although I will give Clem a call. Do you know where I'd like to go, Joss?'

She smiled at him, love shining from her eyes. 'The North Pole is very popular these days.'

'I've never particularly wanted to make love on an ice floe . . . although when you smile at me like that I'd make love anywhere at all.' He grinned at her boyishly. 'You've made me forget my train of thought.'

'Our destination,' she prompted.

'As long as we're together it doesn't really matter, does it? I love you so much, Joss.' He put down his suitcase, took her in his arms and kissed her, and the ever-moving crowds of travellers, used to meetings and farewells, eddied casually around them.

'We're free, aren't we?' Joss whispered dazedly.

'Free of the past, free to be together. Niall, I'm so happy, it almost frightens me.'

'You don't have to be frightened—because no matter what happens we'll go through it together.' He gave her a quick squeeze. 'Let's see if we can get a flight to Nova Scotia so I can meet your parents.'

Her whole face lit up. 'Niall, that's a wonderful idea! There's nothing I'd like better.'

But the only available bookings would not get them into Halifax until nine that night. Joss said dubiously, 'It's a two-and-a-half-hour drive from the airport to the farm.'

'We could stay in Halifax overnight,' Niall said steadily.

Her lashes dropped to hide her eyes. She would like that, too. But, remembering the presence of the ticket agent, Joss restricted herself to a sedate, 'That's a good idea.'

Niall paid for the tickets, then placed a call to Clem. Joss waited a short distance from the row of telephones, deciding privately that she adored the way Niall's hair curled on the nape of his neck. He talked for a while, made a second call, then came back to Joss.

'I got hold of Clem. When I told him the doctors figured I'd be around another fifty years or so, he said that would just about give him time to whip me into shape. I also told him I wouldn't be back for a couple of days. He wanted to know if you were with me, and sent his regards.' Niall gave her his crooked smile. 'The final barrier to our marriage is removed—Clem approves of you.'

Joss laughed. 'I can't believe he only sent his regards.'

'I wouldn't dream of exposing your maidenly ears to what he actually did say.' Niall's eyes were very blue. 'I reserved a suite in Halifax's most expensive hotel, as well . . . after all those years of medical training you can still blush, Joss.'

She scowled at him. 'A suite sounds very extravagant.'

'We've waited six years.' Niall looked at his watch. 'At the moment, six hours sounds like an impossibly long wait.'

'We could go to the observation lounge and watch the planes,' she suggested limpidly.

'Or we could play video games.'

She winced. 'Or toast our future at the bar.'

'Best idea yet,' he said promptly.

They wandered around the airport until flight-time, trying on silly hats in the souvenir shops, chuckling at the books of cartoons and generally, thought Joss, behaving like a couple of children. She had seen little of Niall's playful side. As they munched on gooey doughnuts in a café she said, 'I'm seeing a whole new side to you.'

He said simply, 'It's because I'm happy, Joss.'

'We've waited a long time for that, too, haven't we?'

'We'll make up for lost time,' Niall said confidently. 'Starting tonight.'

She could feel herself blushing again. 'I haven't even got a suitcase.'

'You don't need one. All I want is you.'

Joss hesitated, for the first time feeling afraid. 'But I've never——'

He covered her sticky fingers with his palm. 'Darling, I know you haven't. Don't be frightened. I'll be as good to you as I know how.'

She was very finely tuned to Niall. She said vigorously, although her cheeks were still red, 'I want you, don't have any doubts about that.'

He threw back his head and laughed. 'That's one of the things I love about you—you always speak your mind. Everything will be fine, you'll see.'

Joss was reassured by his words. But at ten-thirty that night, when she followed the bellboy into the suite in Halifax's most expensive hotel, she was filled with an unsettling mixture of excitement and panic. While the bellboy showed Niall the various amenities of the three rooms, she wandered over to the window, which overlooked the calm black waters of the harbour on which were reflected the golden lights of Dartmouth, Halifax's twin city. There was an oil rig moored near the other shore. She studied it with intense interest.

After a discreet rustle of bills, the door to the suite closed and Niall slipped the chain into place. He said, 'Would you like me to order room service, Joss? Are you hungry?'

They had had an indifferent meal on the plane. 'No, thanks,' she replied, turning round to face him, wishing she did not feel quite so much at bay.

'Why don't you have a hot bath? There's complimentary shampoo and bubble bath.'

'I haven't even got a housecoat!'

'You can borrow mine,' he said with ineffable patience.

He was very carefully keeping his distance from her, and suddenly she was furious with herself for worrying about housecoats when she and Niall were finally alone together. She walked over to him, locked her arms around his waist and said in a rush, 'Niall, take me to bed.'

His answer was to switch out the overhead light so that the room was lit only indirectly by the glow from the city, and then to take her by the hand and lead her to the bed. He pulled back the covers. 'Sit down and I'll take off your shoes,' he said matter-of-factly.

As he knelt in front of her, easing her feet from her pumps, his bent head filled Joss with tenderness. Then he kicked off his own shoes and shrugged out of his jacket before drawing her down on the bed beside him and saying softly, 'We've waited a long time for this, as well.'

'Too long.' Her smile was radiant and very trusting. 'I love you more than any one else in the world, Niall.'

'You are my heart's delight,' he said huskily.

He made love to her with gentleness and passion, with infinite care for her pleasure and yet with a fierce hunger. And she, who had waited so long, was glad she had waited, so that she could learn with Niall the intricate and beautiful dance of love. When it was over she was lying across his chest, her cheek resting on his breastbone where his heartbeat echoed in her ear, her arm curving round his scarred ribs to hold him close. 'I never want to let you go,' she murmured. 'Niall, that was wonderful. I'm glad you were the first one.' Realising the implications of what she had said, she gave a throaty chuckle. 'You'll also be the second and the third, I trust.'

'Give me five minutes.'

'According to what I learned in class about male sexuality——' she broke off as he began tickling her ribs. 'Stop that!'

'I bet your textbooks never described some of the things we just did,' he said complacently.

'Fourth Year Eroticism? It wasn't part of the curriculum.'

'One should always be open to new learning.'

'Indeed,' she replied. Then she suddenly sat up, forgetful of her nakedness, her face agitated. 'Niall, I have a confession to make!'

He clasped his hands behind his head in a way that emphasised, to her secret pleasure, the taut concavity of his belly, and said lazily, 'You had triplets at the age of fourteen.'

'I was madly in love with the Enwright boys at the age of fourteen,' she admitted. 'But they were only interested in playing baseball. Niall, while I was away I went to see your father.'

'In Vancouver?' he said incredulously.

'I have a sister there, so I stayed with her. He told me about your mother's illness.'

Even more incredulously Niall said, 'He actually talked to you about her?'

'Yes . . . I think he'd like to talk to you about her, too.'

'Her illness was always a barrier . . . Joss, I've got a hell of a lot of explaining to do.'

'You don't have to explain anything,' she assured him, curling up against his side and running her fingers through the tangle of his body hair.

'I owe you something for the past six years.' He brought her hand to his lips. 'Do you know what made me change my mind last week? The thought that because I was too stubborn or too afraid to claim you, you'd marry Bryan. The Thursday before the wedding I couldn't stand it any longer. I called St David's and was informed by the secretary that the wedding had been cancelled. Not postponed. Cancelled.' He kissed her fingers one by one. 'I knew then I'd been given a third chance. I'd muffed the first two, but I sure wasn't going to mess up the third. So I started phoning you.'

'I left Thursday morning.'

'I finally extracted that piece of information from your superintendent when I turned up on Friday loaded with flowers and a proposal of marriage. He didn't approve of me at all. Kept telling me you were engaged to a doctor with a BMW.'

She said shrewdly, 'How much did it cost you to get into my apartment?'

'You're not supposed to ask. Anyway, I left the flowers and went home, and answered the phone on the first ring for the next three days.' He smiled at her. 'I have no doubt the delay was character-building. But, my God, I missed you.'

'When I got back from Vancouver yesterday, the first thing I did was go to your place. Which you'd already left. We should both have strong characters, Niall.'

He smoothed a strand of hair from her forehead. 'I

can tell you about my mother's illness now. I never could before.'

'Your father told me quite a bit about it. You see, once I'd broken my engagement and sent back all the presents, I couldn't stand being in Toronto. I'd managed to winkle your father's address out of Clem. So I went to Vancouver and on Monday had tea with him . . . I so badly needed to understand you!'

'I was running scared,' Niall said grimly. 'You have no idea what it was like growing up in that huge old house with the servants and my father all behaving as if everything was normal and my poor mother wandering around like a lost soul . . . sometimes she didn't even know who I was. One day I saw her turn on my father with a vegetable knife.' His smile was wry. 'A vegetable knife. Doesn't sound like much, does it? But his hands were bleeding by the time he got it from her, and then she collapsed on the floor sobbing hysterically . . . I've never forgotten that.'

'And no one ever told you what was going on?'

'No. I understand now, of course. But I was left with a terror of illness, not so much for myself as for the ones around me. Since I was a kid I've known what it's like to watch someone you love suffer. I decided a long time ago I'd never put anyone through that. I couldn't have told you the truth six years ago, Joss, not for anything—and even when I met you again, I wanted the check-up out of the way before I made any kind of commitment.'

She rested her head on one hand looking down at him. 'You'd never disappear again, would you, Niall?'

'Never—I swear. I did a lot of thinking over the week-end, remembering that boy in the old house and realising that it was past time to let him go, that he'd been running my life for too long. I thought a lot about love too, Joss—love for better or for worse. You and I will love each other always, no matter what happens . . . I'd swear to that, too.'

'Then we're safe,' Joss whispered.

'Would you be content living in Braxton? We could keep an apartment in Toronto while you're working at the clinic.'

'Maybe I could eventually set up a practice in Braxton.'

'You always were a country girl at heart . . . I've wondered if that's why I bought the place, because I knew we were destined to meet again.'

'How terrible if we hadn't,' Joss said shakily, pressing close to his naked body.

'We had to. We were meant for each other. And we have a whole lifetime ahead of us to prove it.' With a spark of fire in his blue eyes, Niall began stroking the swell of her breast. 'Starting right now.'

'So the five minutes are over?' she asked innocently.

He slid his lips along the white skin that his fingers had been caressing. 'There's a great deal more that the textbooks omitted.'

'Teach me, Niall,' Joss said huskily. 'Teach me.'

Early the next afternoon Joss led Niall into the kitchen of the farmhouse in Alderney and said, 'Mum, I've brought the right man home.'

Harlequin Presents

Coming Next Month

1183   **HEAT OF THE MOMENT Lindsay Armstrong**
Serena's first encounter with Sean Wentworth is embarrassing—so she's surprised to get the job of looking after his nephews at his remote Queensland station. Her relationship with Sean is just beginning to blossom when the past catches up with her.

1184   **TRUE PARADISE Catherine George**
If Roberto Monteiro chooses to think Charlotte used her female charms to gain her own—or her father's—ends, let him. Once he leaves the neighborhood she needn't see him again. Then Roberto insists that Charlotte come to Brazil with the contract....

1185   **STORMY ATTRACTION Madeleine Ker**
Paula prepares to do everything she can to keep the small island paradise off Majorca from development. She hadn't known her opponent would be charming Juan Torres—or that her heart would be at war with her convictions!

1186   **THE THIRD KISS Joanna Mansell**
Separated from her holiday group in Egypt, Bethan is rescued by Max Lansdelle. Only after she blackmails him into letting her stay in his camp does she realize that Max is not the cool customer she thought he was.

1187   **PRISONER OF THE MIND Margaret Mayo**
Lucy blames arrogant businessman Conan Templeton for her father's death and is horrified when she has to act as his secretary. So why is she disappointed when theirs seems likely to remain only a business relationship?

1188   **A QUESTION OF LOVE Annabel Murray**
Keir Trevelyan finally tracks down his dead brother's child, but Venna isn't going to give up her half sister's daughter that easily. She pretends to be a reckless mother with loose morals. Naturally, she's trapped by her own deception....

1189   **WHITE MIDNIGHT Kathleen O'Brien**
Amanda is desperate to be rid of Drake Daniels when he invades her family's Georgia estate, flaunting his new wealth. She once gave him everything—and paid the price.

1190   **A DIFFERENT DREAM Frances Roding**
Lucilla Bellaire wants success and is prepared to go to any lengths for it—or so she thinks. When Nicholas Barrington is neither bowled over by her beauty nor repelled by her ruthlessness, she faces a situation she can't cope with.

Available in July wherever paperback books are sold, or through Harlequin Reader Service:

In the U.S.
901 Fuhrmann Blvd.
P.O. Box 1397
Buffalo, N.Y. 14240-1397

In Canada
P.O. Box 603
Fort Erie, Ontario
L2A 5X3

Janet DAILEY

THE MASTER FIDDLER

Jacqui didn't want to go back to college, and she didn't want to go home. Tombstone, Arizona, wasn't in her plans, either, until she found herself stuck there en route to L.A. after ramming her car into rancher Choya Barnett's Jeep. Things got worse when she lost her wallet and couldn't pay for the repairs. The mechanic wasn't interested when she practically propositioned him to get her car back—but Choya was. He took care of her bills and then waited for the debt to be paid with the only thing Jacqui had to offer—her virtue.

Watch for this bestselling Janet Dailey favorite, coming in June from Harlequin.

Also watch for *Something Extra* in August and *Sweet Promise* in October.

JAN-MAS-1

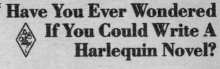

Have You Ever Wondered If You Could Write A Harlequin Novel?

Here's great news—Harlequin is offering a series of cassette tapes to help you do just that. Written by Harlequin editors, these tapes give practical advice on how to make your characters—and your story— come alive. There's a tape for each contemporary romance series Harlequin publishes.

Mail order only

All sales final

TO: *Harlequin Reader Service*
**Audiocassette Tape Offer
P.O. Box 1396
Buffalo, NY 14269-1396**

I enclose a check/money order payable to HARLEQUIN READER SERVICE® for $9.70 ($8.95 plus 75¢ postage and handling) for EACH tape ordered for the total sum of $_____*
Please send:

☐ Romance and Presents   ☐ Intrigue
☐ American Romance   ☐ Temptation
☐ Superromance   ☐ All five tapes ($38.80 total)

Signature_____
                                          (please print clearly)
Name:_____
Address:_____
State:_____ Zip:_____

*Iowa and New York residents add appropriate sales tax.

AUDIO-H

ANNOUNCING . . .

The Lost Moon Flower
by Bethany Campbell

**Look for it this August
wherever Harlequins are sold**

HR 3000-1